WOLF RANCH: ROUGH

WOLF RANCH - BOOK 1

RENEE ROSE
VANESSA VALE

Wolf Ranch: Rough

Copyright © 2020 by Bridger Media and Wilrose Dream Ventures LLC

This is a work of fiction. Names, characters, places and incidents are the products of the author's imagination and used fictitiously. Any resemblance to actual persons, living or dead, businesses, companies, events or locales is entirely coincidental.

All rights reserved.

No part of this book may be reproduced in any form or by any electronic or mechanical means, including information storage and retrieval systems, without written permission from both authors, except for the use of brief quotations in a book review.

Cover design: Bridger Media

Cover graphic: Period Images; Deposit Photos: tolstnev

WANT FREE RENEE ROSE BOOKS?

Go to http://subscribepage.com/alphastemp to sign up for Renee Rose's newsletter and receive a free copy of *Alpha's Temptation*, *Theirs to Protect, Owned by the Marine, Theirs to Punish, The Alpha's Punishment, Disobedience at the Dressmaker's* and *Her Billionaire Boss*. In addition to the free stories, you will also get bonus epilogues, special pricing, exclusive previews and news of new releases.

GET A FREE VANESSA VALE BOOK!

Join Vanessa's mailing list to be the first to know of new releases, free books, special prices and other author giveaways.

http://freeromanceread.com

1

OYD

My thoughts were on fucking.

Most guys had their heads focused on their upcoming ride, the eight seconds they had to keep their ass on the back of a pissed off bull. Me? I wasn't thinking with *that* head.

I was amped up, and I wanted to pump that excess energy into a hot, tight pussy. And there were tons of options around the arena.

"Hey, champ. Can't wait to see you ride," one of the buckle bunnies cooed as she strutted past me.

"Thanks, gorgeous." All I had to do was wink at Sherry or Cindy... whatever her name was, and I could take *her* for a ride. With the jean skirt that was—thank you baby Jesus— nothing more than a denim Band-Aid around her waist and a white tank top that barely hid her perky tits, I knew what was on offer. The ride might take longer than eight seconds

—I could go all night—but once I climbed off, like with a bull, I didn't linger. The ladies knew the score. I got off—got them off a time or two since I was a gentleman—and they could brag they'd fucked the rodeo champ. Everyone left satisfied.

Satisfied, definitely. Happy? Not so much anymore. Sure, Sherry/Cindy was gorgeous, but a romp with the lollipop of the day didn't do that much for me anymore.

Or for my wolf. A quick lay wasn't what we wanted. Maybe it was the start of moon madness kicking in, but it was pissing me off. My dick had become... selective. That's what happened to shifters who were ready to mate. Their inner wolf sought a true mate, and no other female would do. That was a big problem for a guy like me who had fucking on his mind... all the time.

The noise from the crowd in the stands was muted on the lower level of the arena. The scent of popcorn and spilled beer couldn't cover the tang from the animals. The concrete floor had scattered bits of hay that clung to my sturdy boots, but I wasn't heading toward the chutes. Not yet. With the steer roping event happening now, I had time to check on my friend, Abe, before my turn in the bull riding event. I turned down a narrow hall and ducked into the medical room.

"Fucker, you hurt your hand before you even got in the ring? What were you doing, jerking off?" I asked, pulling my hat off as I came in the door.

Then I stopped short. Froze. *Holy fuck.*

My wolf perked up. Sniffed.

Yeah, Abe was sitting on an exam table in his dusty jeans and snap shirt, but I wasn't looking at him. Hell, he could have been wearing a hula outfit, and I wouldn't have known. It was the woman who was holding his hand, putting some kind of metal brace around his finger, who I stared at.

Petite, curvy and with the most luscious ass, she could make a man weep... or jizz in his jeans like a fifteen-year-old. My wolf stood up and preened. She looked my way with wide eyes behind glasses. Fuck me, I had no idea I had a thing for glasses. My usual woman ran tall and willowy, with perky tits that overflowed in the palms of my hands. Maybe that was where my problem lay, where my selectiveness came from. None of them were *her*.

But that didn't make sense. I didn't need to breathe in to pick up her scent. In the small room, the sweet aroma of ripe peaches hit me like a stampeding bull.

Delicious. But not the scent of a she-wolf.

She was human. A gorgeous, curvy, human.

My wolf practically howled at the sight of her. Long hair cascaded down her back like a dark waterfall. She had a round face with skin as pale as cream. Her plump lips would look incredible wrapped around my dick. And those curves. Oh fuck, yes. Tits that would fit perfectly in my hands, wide hips that would be perfect to grab as I fucked her from behind. And that ass? Yeah, I couldn't miss those delectable curves since she faced Abe but was glancing over her shoulder at me. That ass would cushion my hips as I pounded into her. It'd also look damned gorgeous with my pink handprints on it.

My dick punched against my jeans wanting to get to her. Get in her.

"What the hell, Boyd?" Abe muttered. "I broke my fucking—sorry, ma'am—finger helping Burt with his tow hitch." He glanced up at the woman, chagrined for saying a bad word. And *ma'am*? What the hell? He was behaving like a blushing school boy with his first crush.

Oh, fuck no. Abe wasn't getting his hands on her. He was human and a decent guy. Still, no fucking way.

"The doc here's bracing it, so I can compete."

Doc? She was a doctor? Maybe I expected a guy in a white lab coat and pressed khakis, not a hot little number like her. A hot *smart* number. She probably had more brains in her left pinky finger than I did in my whole head. All I knew was she was mine.

She deftly wound some white medical tape around the braced finger and the one beside it, securing them together, then tore off the strip. He'd lucked out it wasn't the hand he used to grip the rope, so he could compete.

"What are you doing later? Think I can buy you a cup of coffee to thank you?" With Abe sitting on the exam table, they were the same height. All he had to do was lean, and he'd be able to kiss her. She eyed Abe, and I wanted to growl, then rip his head off.

"I won't be able to concentrate without knowing your answer."

"Focus less on me and more on that bull you have to ride."

Abe grinned, that smile a known lethal weapon to women's panties.

I launched myself forward, tugged off my cowboy hat and stuck my hand out. "Hey there, I'm Boyd."

She glanced my way, then back to her work. Her gloved fingers wound one more strip around Abe's fingers. "Hi, Boyd. Sorry—my hands are full."

Blue. Her eyes were blue behind those nerdy, fuck-me glasses.

"Oh, ah. Right." I dropped my hand and settled instead for my own panty-dropping smile. The one that usually guaranteed me a woman's phone number without having to ask for it. I stepped closer, close enough that Abe frowned.

Mine, buddy. Back the fuck off.

"I'm Doctor Ames—Audrey. Excuse me." She needed me to step back because I nearly had her pinned against the table with my body. Not touching, but definitely crowding.

"Audrey Ames," I repeated. "Guess you always got the first desk in school."

"Yep, you know it." She didn't look at me twice. Didn't blush or bat her eyelashes. Didn't stick out her chest, so I could see what was on offer. Hell, she hardly did more than glance my way once more as she moved to the counter where she made notes in a file.

"Doc here works at a hospital but is moonlighting the event in case someone gets hurt," Abe explained, holding up his injured hand.

I frowned. "You know her shoe size and what she had for breakfast this morning, too?"

Audrey spun about and gave me a look that would have withered the balls on a lesser man. Still, it was far from the *fuck me now* expression I was used to. "I'm standing right here."

I winked and looked her up and down. "You sure are."

After a quick purse of her lips, she tugged off her gloves and tossed them in the trash can.

Goddamn. The first time a female had truly interested me in years—maybe ever—and she barely saw me. Didn't give a shit that the big buckle on my belt meant I was a rodeo champion. Didn't give a shit that the dick pressed uncomfortably right behind it was rock hard just for her.

How was that even possible?

I ignored the hairy eyeball Abe threw my way.

"Why haven't I seen you around before?" I tried again.

"Me?" She looked over, surprised. Like I came in here to flirt with Abe or something.

"As Abe said, I work at Community General in Cooper Valley, and unless you were going to have a baby, we'd never meet. Your regular rodeo doc had something come up, so they called our hospital begging for a fill-in to cover tonight. The pay was decent, and I have med school loans, so I figured, why not?" She shrugged. "I've always wanted to see a rodeo."

Of course, I never got hurt, or if I did, not enough to ever need a hospital since shifters healed so fast.

"Sorry, sweetheart," Abe said, his eyes going up to the ceiling as if he could see through to the stands above us. "I've messed up your spectator plans."

She gave him a small smile. *Him.* Why the fuck didn't she offer me one of those soft turn of her lips?

"I'll get up there after this and see you ride."

Abe's chest puffed up, and I wanted to break the rest of his fingers. Better yet, his leg, so he couldn't compete. If she was going to see someone ride a bull, it was going to be me.

"*You* live in Cooper Valley." I hardly believed the coincidence. "You gotta be kidding me."

She finally gave me her full attention, turning and leaning that gorgeous ass against the cabinet to look at me with curiosity. "Yes. I moved here a little while ago. Why?"

I pointed at my chest. "I'm *from* Cooper Valley—Wolf Ranch. You know it?"

She shook her head, her dark hair sliding over her shoulders. "No, I'm fairly new to town and work tons of hours. I know the inside of the hospital really well." She gave me a wry smile.

There. A fucking smile. I was like a beggar seeking the smallest of crumbs from her.

I sidled in her direction. "I could take a day or two off and show you around. Love to, in fact."

Abe cleared his throat, making Audrey look his way. "You're all set," she told him. "Don't break anything else out there. I have no idea how you guys do it."

He hopped down off the table, picked up his hat and settled it on his head. He didn't make a move to leave. Hell no. He was trying to make a *move*.

The asshole had the nerve to grin, then slap my back with his good hand, much harder than necessary. "Well, we'd better get into the chutes. Almost time for the bull rides. You gonna watch me, Doc?"

I gave him a look that screamed *fuck off, she's mine*. I might've even growled a little, too.

We had a short stare down, and he finally relented. He sighed, flicked the rim of his hat. "Ma'am."

I knew Abe was a smart guy because he finally left, and I was alone with the hottest female in all of Montana.

"About that tour," I said, taking a step closer and giving her my easygoing smile. I tucked my thumbs into my front pockets.

I wasn't the kinda guy who believed in signs or gave much credence to fate, but after my wolf's reaction to her presence, to discover such a gorgeous creature was living in my hometown felt significant. After all the wandering the fucking country riding angry bulls, and she'd been right fucking here. It was fate the rodeo was in my hometown, and she was working it.

"Oh, no," she dismissed me immediately, turning away to clean up from tending to Abe. "I'll watch the bull riding and see you and Abe ride but have to go right back to work when I go home. Thanks, though."

Shot down. It was just a tour. Sure, it meant I wanted to

show her around... my dick, but I'd show her a few sights first. Maybe she needed to see me in action. First on the back of a bull, then maybe in bed. Who didn't want to fuck the champion? It wasn't like I had anything to worry about. No human could out-ride me. Especially not when I wanted to win.

I definitely wanted to win now. I stuffed my hat back on my head.

Doctor Audrey wanted to see some riding? I would show her exactly how it was done.

2

UDREY

THE TESTOSTERONE in the arena was overwhelming.

Unfortunately, my undersexed body was standing up and taking notice. I would swear my ovaries dropped two eggs when Boyd entered the med room. All cowboy swagger and charm. He'd stepped so close I'd been able to smell his aftershave and soap, and it did something crazy to my head. I mean, my body. Everywhere. I got all hot and tingly, and my brain lost power for the moment.

I already had a thing for cowboys. The hats, the loose hipped gait, rugged exteriors and the air of... *maleness*. It was definitely a perk of moving to Montana. Boyd was about as gorgeous as God made them with that chiseled jaw and lazy smile. Sandy colored hair that was a few weeks past a haircut. Pale eyes that had roved over me as if I were a tasty treat he wanted to devour. A crooked nose that proved while he might be quick with the smile, he was probably quick with the fists, too. It was the whole package—all six feet plus of pure muscle and virile man that made my nipples harden and my panties get damp.

My body had reacted to his presence like I'd been seeping in pheromones that crazily enough made me feel like I was in heat, and he was some kind of stallion ready to mount. I might not have been with a man in a while... close to a few days short of forever, but I knew the signs. He'd wanted me as another notch on his bedpost.

My mind was a total slut—wanting to be tied to that notched bedpost—which it had no business being. The animals might be branded, but each one of those Grade-A cowboys should have a mark that guaranteed them players. They were all quick-grinning males who could make a woman wet with just a wink and have her drop her panties with the crook of a finger.

These rodeo champs apparently thought they were God's gift to women, although why Boyd and Abe—Abe might have been subtle about his intentions, but he'd flirted nonetheless— bothered making a play for me when there were a dozen or more scantily dressed cowgirls out there for the taking was beyond me. They probably dished it out to every female they met. Cowboy code or something. My panties were ruined after being in the same room as Boyd for even a few short minutes, but I fortunately still had them on. Or, unfortunately, because I had no doubt the guy knew his way around a woman's body, and there'd been a perfectly sturdy exam table for me to be bent over and fucked.

Yup, my slutty mind was pretty darned busy. Abe was the only injury so far for the event, and I was able to head to the stands and watch the bull riding. I was the doctor on call. If someone got hurt, I was to tend to them, connect with the ambulance standing by and get the person to the hospital.

From where I sat—unless someone randomly started choking on a corn dog in the vendor area—I'd know if my assistance was needed. I sat near the aisle with easy access to the competitor area and a great view of the chutes. This was where the bulls were held and readied, then the cowboy climbed the fence and hopped on its back. Once the man was secure, the gate was flung open and off they went, the pissed off bull doing anything to fling off his rider. It practically guaranteed me a few more patients before the event was over.

I scanned the chute area for the two of them, watched as the first few competitors completed their rides. I was equally turned on and filled with dread as one after another had his turn. The crowd felt the same as me, cheering and gasping in equal measure. Riding a bull was the sexiest thing I'd ever seen. And the dumbest.

I didn't know how these guys lived past thirty. Maybe they didn't. That thought made my chest unexpectedly tighten, like I'd already developed an attachment to the two cowboys I'd met.

Not the first one, the second. Abe was handsome. Gentle, considering his size and what he did for a living. Sweet, even. Boyd, though, was... dangerous. I wasn't afraid he would hurt me physically, although he had at least a foot on me and probably fifty pounds, but something else. He could hurt my heart. Screw with my plans. I'd been so focused on med school and my residency. On my career. It wasn't like me to deviate because of a perfect ass in a pair of Wranglers. He was a bad boy who I knew was trouble but wanted anyway.

A rider was flung from his bull and landed hard, then

rolled to clear himself from the back hooves of the bull. The rodeo clowns—I was sure they had some other name I didn't know—ran over, redirected the animal, so the rider could get to his feet. I exhaled as the crowd cheered at his high score. He dusted himself off, lifted his hat in salute and walked out of the ring.

Boyd's face appeared on the jumbotron, his quick smile twenty feet wide. The crowd went wild, which meant his ego was probably as big as his image on the huge screen. Yeah, I needed to keep my distance from that one because I wasn't the one-night-stand kind of woman. With med school and residency, I barely socialized, let alone dated, let alone had tons of sex. Or any, really. Maybe a fling would be best for my crazy schedule, but no, that wasn't me. I was the long term, commitment type. In fact, I'd moved to small town Montana to settle down. Slow down. Find a partner and start a family, just as I'd always longed to have. A family made up of two parents who loved each other and a gaggle of kids. I wanted that kind of insanity. Sledding, science fair projects, pet gerbils. That was what I longed for. Especially babies.

Screwing a rodeo champ was not part of that picture, and I doubted a rodeo champ wanted to fuck a woman who had baby fever. The words "ticking clock" wasn't the same for him as it was for me. His plans lasted eight seconds, mine a lifetime.

Still, my body went on full alert when I spied his name on the ticker—Boyd Wolf vs. Night Sweats, which was a crazy name for a bull.

I leaned forward to spot him down in the chutes. They all looked the same in their helmets, safety vests and chaps, the sponsors' logos splashed across the shoulders of their collared button-downs. But then I saw him—at least I was fairly certain it was him. The rider oozed the same raw confidence he'd shown in the medical room.

He straddled the snorting black bull then set about adjusting his grip on the rope with easy, deft movements. Only his hand held him on that beast. I knew none of the details about bull riding, only that I'd overheard it was called a rough stock event. *Rough* was the definitely right word.

"Hey, pretty lady." Abe came up the concrete steps and settled his large body into the seat beside me.

I couldn't help but smile at him, but I glanced back at the chutes.

"Hard to watch?" he asked.

I nodded. "Your ride went well. You stayed on past the buzzer. I should be congratulating you, right?"

He tipped his hat back, then set his hand on my shoulder. "Yes, ma'am. Best ride of the night. So far. We can celebrate by you getting that coffee with me after."

His quick grin and mild manner had me smiling. He was handsome. Courteous. But like Jett Markle, the local rancher who I'd had one bad date with the week before, he didn't do anything for me. Like those romance novels I read in my spare time, I wanted spark. Heat. Attraction. *Chemistry.*

Jett was turning out to be a creep, so I couldn't put Abe into the same category.

The announcer called the next ride, and I was distracted by Boyd's imminent turn. When I looked his way again, he wasn't focused on the thousand pounds of pissed off animal beneath him, but at me. His gaze was locked onto me, and I gasped. No, he wasn't looking at me, but at Abe's hand on my shoulder. Boyd's jaw clenched, his eyes narrowed. If I wasn't mistaken, he was as pissed off by that action as the bull was to have a rider sitting on him.

Why was he looking at me? I wasn't important. I was the short, dumpy doctor who had zero social life. Still, he stared. I tried to school my breath when he nodded his head. I realized it wasn't for me when the chute was flung open.

Night Sweats came pawing out, snorting with fury over the rider on his back. I held my breath, stomach bunched up in a tight knot as he kicked his back legs up.

Even with the wild ride, Boyd seemed to take the body-snapping movements with ease, his thighs gripping the sides of the bull, his arm flung up, his back staying loose, his movements gracefully in sync with the animal.

It was mesmerizing.

Magical, even.

A wide smile stretched across his lips like riding bulls was a walk in the park for him. Oh God. Was that for real?

He scanned the audience... as he rode the bull.

What bull rider had the presence of mind to look for Mom when he was trying to stay on the back of a pissed off bull?

The crowd was going wild—cheering and stamping. Boyd had already been on the bull for eight seconds.

Nine.

I stood to see better, and he caught sight of me. Again.

That was impossible.

He might have glanced my way before, but now? On the back of a bull? He wouldn't be looking for me in the crowd.

I shrieked, covering my mouth as he was thrown, flipped straight into the air like a frisbee. Oh God—no! Time slowed. I squeezed my eyes closed, then opened them again at the horror unfolding. As Boyd's spinning body came down, the bull turned and tossed its head, landing a vicious horn right below the protection of Boyd's vest.

He'd been gored.

Badly.

Possibly lethally.

"Oh shit," Abe said. While I knew it wasn't good, Abe's words confirmed it. He'd seen more rides than I had, and this was worse than others.

I switched into medical mode, my training kicking in. I ran down the steps before I even knew my feet were moving, sprinting along with the EMTs for the arena.

"Hold up!" a manager yelled, barring our entrance while the rodeo clowns distracted the bull, and two riders rode out to rope it. "Now, go! Go!"

Boyd was on one knee, trying to get to his feet. Adrenaline was probably the only thing keeping him upright. Blood soaked his shirt and jeans, staining the dirt below him.

"Stop moving!" I yelled as I ran up. "Hold still, Boyd." To the EMTs who followed with a backboard, I barked, "Get him on."

Carefully, they transferred him to the board, strapped him to it and stood, walking quickly across the dirt ring toward where they'd left the gurney.

"I'm going to need a pressure bandage and an IV. And morphine," I ordered, one of them speaking into the walkie talkie strapped to his shoulder, giving information, hopefully, to the ER. "I'll ride along to the hospital."

I wasn't a trauma doctor. I was an ObGyn, but all my training as I did my rotations came rushing back. I jogged alongside the gurney, trying to gauge the depth, location and severity of the wound when a hand closed on mine.

My gaze flew to Boyd's face. It was pale and sweat stood

out on his forehead, but he grinned at me.

"Just a scratch, Doc," he said, his voice raspy. His breathing was difficult, especially on inhales. I had to assume a punctured lung. "No need to worry."

Was he actually comforting *me*? Now?

I squeezed his hand back, surprised at how relieved his upbeat attitude made me feel. As a doctor, I knew he was in a great deal of danger but was also aware the patient's outlook could make the difference between living and dying.

"I usually do the reassuring, but I'm glad you're staying positive. I'll get you something for the pain as soon as we're in the ambulance."

He winced, trying to sit up and look at the injury.

I pushed him back down, although he wasn't going anywhere with the strap around his waist. "Take it easy, champ, you're losing blood."

He gave a half grin as his face turned pasty. His blood pressure was most likely dropping, and he was going into shock. I needed to get him stabilized right away. As his lashes flickered, he mumbled, "Guess you're not going out with Abe for coffee, huh?"

What? He had a hole in his chest and was worried about me going out with Abe? "Guess not. Hang on for me, okay?"

But it was too late. He'd lost consciousness.

Heart thundering in my chest, I hustled into the ambulance with him and took over the insertion of the IV needle into his arm as the paramedic settled an oxygen mask over his face.

Boyd Wolf was probably the cockiest cowboy in the west. It was his job to get on the back of a bull, but it was my job to save him when he fell off. I'd do everything I possibly could to do so.

3

OYD

I BLINKED, looked around. Where the fuck was I? Sterile walls. Beeping monitors. Antiseptic scent. Shit. No.

I couldn't be in a hospital. I'd barely gotten scratched when that bull nicked me with his horn. It had hurt like fucking hell, but it hadn't been so bad. Just a little blood loss. A big hole in my chest. I'd seen Audrey in the stands—my wolf ready to show off for her—and was prepared to focus on the ride, all eight plus seconds, and then get back to her. Get *in* her. But then I'd seen Abe set his hand on her shoulder, and I'd focused on that. The way his fingers lightly gripped her. Felt her heat, could breathe in her sweet scent. I'd thought of that, only that. Not the big ass bull I'd been riding on.

Was she interested in Abe? Had she liked his touch? I'd wondered about that, then I'd been pissed as hell. *No fucking way.* My wolf had screamed at me, "He's touching her! Get his fucking hands off her. Now!"

Abe would've had more than a broken finger before the night was out, an entire hand, except the bull had kicked just right, and I'd gone flying. I was used to falling off. Hell, I did it on purpose often enough, so people wouldn't wonder as to why I was so fucking daring. It was the fact I knew I'd never get hurt that made me champ. Even a horn in my torso couldn't keep me down for long.

What was bad, and sad, was that I'd fucking passed out. I'd planned on jumping off that gurney before it ever made it into the ambulance, track down Abe and tell him he could fucking forget Audrey even existed.

Not that Doctor Blue-Eyes would've let that happen. She'd been there within seconds of me hitting the hard packed dirt and began to treat me as if I were human.

She'd touched me. I'd felt it through the pain. My wolf had, too.

Hell, if getting her to focus on me was to get gored by a fucking bull, I should have done it earlier in the night. I remembered her squeezing my hand as she jogged beside the board they'd strapped me to. Vaguely, I remembered her next to me in the ambulance, speaking in those low, clipped tones to the EMTs. Stern. Authoritative. Bossy as fuck. That little slip of a female had given orders like the most ruthless of alphas.

I was good at sensing people. It was the shifter in me. Audrey had been worried... about *me*. And I remembered liking how that felt. She cared and if that didn't do something funny to my insides.

I fought the drugs pumping through my veins and opened my eyes once again. I had no idea how long I'd been out and that was bad. My body was healing wolf-quick, and anyone could have noticed. I knew exactly nothing about hospitals since this was the first time I'd been in one, but it looked like they were going to do some kind of procedure, maybe even take me to the operating room. Watching doctor shows on TV clued me in to that possibility. A nurse in blue scrubs had her back to me, arranging instruments on a tray, then stepped out of the room. Like whatever was planned was going to happen.

I stifled a groan as I tugged the IV needle out of my arm and disconnected the monitoring equipment.

The last thing I needed was to expose my species to human doctors, especially the ones in my own home town. Revealing what we were was against pack rules. The easiest way to do that was to get them to cut me open.

My brother Rob—the pack alpha—would kill me. He'd do it in a more painful way than being gored, that was for fucking sure. He already thought I was a fuck-up and would probably swear up one side of Sunday and back down the other for getting injured in front of an entire arena full of people and forced to have medical intervention.

If he were me, he would have gone off into the woods, shifted and licked his wounds until he was healed, which would have taken a few short hours.

Me? Yeah, I was in fucking trouble here.

As softly as I could, I rolled off the hospital bed to crouch on the floor. A hospital gown had been draped over my privates and fell to the floor. I had to assume they hadn't put me in it so they could keep my chest exposed, so they could treat it. I was bare ass naked. Picking the gown up, I shoved my arms through the sleeves. My ass was hanging out, and I was too weak and groggy to reach back and tie the tabs closed, probably more from the morphine than from the wound. I gave my head a shake to clear it.

I looked down and touched the place on my chest the bull had punctured. I couldn't see it through the scratchy fabric, but I could feel that the flesh had closed. It was well on its way to healing, thank fuck. Even an injury as grave as a fucking bull horn through my chest knitted and fused fast. Quickly, before the nurse returned, I slipped out the door, the back of my gown flapping open in the back. I didn't give a shit if someone saw my bare ass. I just wanted out.

I opened the cabinets outside my room until I found the plastic bag with my bloodied clothing and personal items and ducked into a bathroom to pull on the crusty clothing. They weren't ideal, but beggars couldn't be choosers. My hat sat on top, and I set it upon my head. I didn't like being without it. I felt more naked with my head bare than in the hospital gown with my butt hanging out.

I dipped my head as I slipped out, but I snapped it up the moment I stepped into the hall and caught her scent. I sniffed. Peaches and vanilla. Yeah, I'd recognize her anywhere. But where was—

I turned to search for her, and she barreled into my arms. Well, my chest, really. That hurt like a bitch, but I caught her elbows to steady her as we collided, my wolf celebrating her nearness. *Mine!*

I smiled down at her, so caught off guard by the intense pleasure of touching her, I forgot my dilemma. I forgot that I was supposed to have a huge hole in my side.

She gasped, then frowned, looked me over. Since she was a full head shorter, her gaze was right at chest level and my bloody, torn shirt. "Boyd! How are you—"

She pulled back to look at my wound, and I dropped my arm from touching her to cover it, hunching a bit like it pained me. I was a bull rider, not an actor, and I was fucking this up more and more by the second.

"Listen, Doc," I began. "I appreciate your help, but I'm more of a heal-at-home kind of guy. Nothing a little time on the couch can't fix. I'm going to check myself out now."

Horror flickered over her face. "You can't!" She reached for the hem of my untucked shirt.

I shrank back. At least, I meant to shrink back. In actuality, something different happened. Her fingertips brushed the skin of my lower belly and every cell in my body reacted. My dick thickened in my jeans.

Shock flashed over her face when I kept her hand from drifting higher to the wound, her pupils narrowing to tiny points, then blowing wide. "But you... I mean—no way. You shouldn't be standing, let alone leaving."

Fuck.

My brain caught up with my dick as soon as it happened, but by then it was too late. I'd wanted to feel her touch, skin to skin. Wanted to feel her heat, to have her scent on me, permeating into me.

Dumb move. *Another* one.

I pushed her hand out from under my shirt and stumbled backward. Running into her was pretty much letting her in on a big fucking secret. A big *shifter* secret.

"I'm ah... not as hurt as you thought. Lots of blood for a little wound. I'm feeling better, but I'll rest up. I promise." I backed up. My wolf howled to stay near her. It didn't understand why I was walking away. "I'm gonna head to my family's ranch. You know, heal."

I had her stunned surprise on my side. It took her seconds to process the unbelievable. At least unbelievable for humans.

"I'll take good care of myself. As long as you promise me you won't go out with Abe. He's not the man for you."

"Wait!" she called, but I'd already turned and started

jogging as swiftly as I could down the hallway. As soon as I turned the corner, I broke into a run and got the fuck out of there as quickly as possible.

Fuck, fuck, fuck.

What had I been thinking? Yeah, I wanted the hot little doc, but I couldn't have her now. There was no fucking way I could even see her again. The secret would be out. I couldn't expose what I was or the pack. Rob would be pissed.

All I could hope was that she didn't realize the extent of healing that had taken place, that I was somehow just a hard-headed bull rider who hated hospitals and that she'd let me go without further inquiry. That I wanted just that. Except... that was a goddamn lie.

She knew who I was. Knew about Wolf Ranch. I'd mentioned where I was from earlier in the arena. I was far from anonymous. If she was as smart as I figured, there was no way she'd take what she'd seen as the end.

No fucking way. She'd come after me. My wolf howled at that. Perhaps that was the only reason why I wasn't running back inside, finding the nearest empty hospital room and fucking her until she had no doubt she was mine and mine alone.

That was the stupidest thing of all. If she showed up at the ranch, I was going to have to explain to Rob—hell, not just Rob but the entire fucking pack—exactly how badly I fucked this up because my wolf was saying Dr. Audrey Ames was my mate.

Yeah, total fucking mess.

As usual.

The black sheep of the family returned.

And he was still the irresponsible playboy everyone thought he was. Plus, his wolf said his mate was human.

4

UDREY

"It was the strangest thing," I said, my eyes on the road.

While I didn't have a fancy car with the in-dashboard phone setup, I did have a stand for my cell and the ability to use the speaker. I was thankful for it since I needed both hands on the steering wheel. The two-lane highway cut through the mountains and followed beside the river, and there were more twists and turns than straightaways. "I saw the accident, saw the wound. Hemothorax, possible ruptured spleen, blood loss."

"I don't know what half of that means, but it sounds bad," Marina said. My sister, well, half-sister, was nine years younger and in college in California. She was no dummy, studying structural engineering, but medicine wasn't her thing.

I frowned, slowed for a curve. "It explains the struggled inhales, the loss of BP. Hmm, maybe it was a spastic diaphragm," I replied, thinking aloud. They were possibilities, but I'd *seen* the accident, the aftermath.

"You said he was standing in the hallway when you ran into him, then walked right out. He had to have been less injured than you thought."

"I *saw* the accident," I repeated. I'd tried to touch his injury, but he'd stopped my hand over his belly. I'd felt the heat of his skin, the hard ridges of his abdomen. What I hadn't felt was a hole in his side. No, I didn't usually get turned on by sucking chest wounds, but it seemed I clearly got all hot and bothered by feeling up a cocky cowboy's torso.

It had been two days since the rodeo, and it was finally my day off. I'd thought about him asking me out, to give me a tour of Cooper Valley. I could've said yes, but I just didn't want to tango with a cowboy who was so obviously a player, no matter how hot he was. Although I was sure he'd be well worth the tumble.

Since then, I'd been busy with patients and a whopping five births—and it wasn't even the full moon—and I'd still thought about Boyd Wolf. I went over every moment of my care for him, from the moment I dropped to my knees in the dirt beside him until I watched his taut ass as he walked out of the hospital. I also thought about the fact that I *had* actually stared at his taut ass. That I thought his ass *was* taut.

It was. Same with his belly. How did I turn into a starry eyed thirteen-year-old having her first crush thinking about a guy non-stop? If it weren't professional, I'd probably have doodled on patient charts little hearts with our names in them.

It was because I was worried about him and because I

thought he was hot that I was in my car and driving to Wolf Ranch where he'd told me he would recover. I also may or may not have contacted the rodeo to make sure he hadn't returned to work. Even if I had overestimated his injuries, he shouldn't have been able to saunter out of the hospital like nothing hurt. Just to be safe, I'd told rodeo management explicitly that he wasn't cleared for competition and shouldn't be allowed to return until he had a full examination.

Preferably by me. Not because I was dying to see those washboard abs in person. Not at all.

"I want to know why you're so bothered," she said. "He wasn't as injured as you thought. This is the first patient..." She cleared her throat. "*Man...* who you've ever thought about going to his house to check on. There's more here."

She might be my baby sister, but she wasn't much of a baby. She knew me well enough to read into my actions. Dammit.

I sped up as the canyon ended and opened up into a wide prairie. I wasn't more than twenty miles from Cooper Valley, but I'd never been on this side of the mountains before. The pines that dotted the rugged canyon disappeared. The land was almost flat, only slight undulations in the landscape. The river curved in the distance, trees lining the bank in spots making it picturesque. *This* was the Montana of my fantasies. Open ranges. Big skies. Vast land and no people.

"Audrey." She prompted me since I'd been quiet as I ogled the view. "Tell me about this hot cowboy."

"I didn't say he was hot," I protested.

She laughed, the sound loud through my cell. "You didn't have to. Please, I have no boyfriend, and there isn't a guy in my program who's even an option. They're more into math equations than breasts. Let me live vicariously through you. What's his name?"

"Boyd Wolf."

She was quiet for a few seconds. "I'm doing a search for him because any guy who lights your fire must be... holy shit, woman. No wonder you're driving to his house. Do you have sexy undies on?"

I gasped, then laughed. "I can't believe you just said that."

I did have on my nicest underwear, a bra and panty set that matched and wasn't made of simple cotton. I also put on makeup, kept my hair down instead of up in a usual sloppy bun and had tried on three different outfits. All for Boyd Wolf. Maybe I really was crazy, putting effort into a guy who was sooooo wrong for me.

"He's not badly injured, you found that out. He's hot as hell, and you touched his abs. Don't you want to touch the rest of him? I'm looking at his pictures online, and I want to lick him from stern to mast."

I rolled my eyes and couldn't help but smile. Marina was twenty-one and single. Someone eighty and married would find him hot.

"There's just something weird about it," I said. "I know what I saw, what I treated. I can't explain it."

It was as if there'd been magic involved. Sleight of hand where you saw a quarter in a hand and the next minute it was in a glass bottle. I saw his wounds. I saw the way he'd been able to hurry out of the hospital a short time later. It made no sense. I couldn't let it go.

"What I want to know is why you're thinking so much about this guy when you had Mr. Hot Rancher on the hook last week."

I frowned. "Who? Jett Markle?"

"From what you told me about him, he's one tall glass of water."

"He's also self-centered, authoritarian and did nothing for me," I grumbled. Jett was thirty-five, handsome in the clean cut, preppy sort of way. His brown hair was parted, well cut and groomed. His smile was broad, but I wondered if it were as fake as the veneers on his teeth. His clothes fit in with Montana. Jeans, simple button-up shirts, leather boots. He was just... polished. Fake. He was playing at being a cowboy whereas Boyd *was* all cowboy.

There I went, using Boyd Wolf as husband measuring stick.

"But Boyd Wolf did."

"Exactly," I replied before I caught myself.

"Ha! I was right. You never told me what happened with Jett."

"We went to a fancy steak place. He ordered for me."

"What?" she practically squawked.

"Yeah, I mean, I don't even like lamb. And rare, yuck! Then he told me about how he'd retired from a hedge fund company at thirty-five and bought a big piece of land to fulfill the lifelong dream of being a rancher."

"Hedge fund company?"

"New York City," I replied.

"Does he actually ranch?"

"I have no idea. I can't imagine him getting his hands dirty let alone riding a horse or castrating calves. He lives on this side of the mountains." I put on my blinker and turned when my GPS said. I'd remembered Boyd mentioning the name of his family property, Wolf Ranch. It wasn't hard to forget when it was his last name. It had been easy to search and plug in for directions. "While most people live in the town, the older homesteads, probably like Wolf Ranch, are over here. Also, the big parcels for the moved-to-Montana folk like Jett."

"So I guess the date was a one-time thing?" she asked. "If he's that bad within the first hour, it's not worth a second go."

I huffed out a laugh. "Yeah, I made it pretty clear I wasn't interested. Didn't even let him walk me to my door. But I think he took it as playing hard to get. Maybe even saving myself." I gave the last mental air quotes. I wasn't a virgin, and I certainly wasn't saving myself for marriage, but I was looking for someone to marry. It just wasn't Jett. I wasn't that bored with my vibrator to sleep with him.

"Why?"

"Because he keeps calling. Even texted and said he'd pick me up on Friday after my shift."

"You told him your work schedule?"

"Hell, no. I have no idea how he got it. Maybe he threw some of his hedge fund money around." I'd been hopeful before the date, but it had been obvious really fast, right about the time he said I'd be eating lamb for dinner, that it wasn't going to happen with Jett. I'd made it clear in my lack of interest, but it bothered me that he didn't grasp the fact that I wasn't interested. He was rich and attractive. Surely there had to be a whole slew of eager women in town to take him on.

The road had followed a split rail fence for the past mile. I slowed when it was broken by a huge archway. If I had any doubts of where I was, the words Wolf Ranch carved into the wood would have helped. The driveway was dirt. Straight. Long. I couldn't see any buildings from the road, which meant the ranch was big.

"Ignore him. Go for Boyd Wolf. If you don't, I will."

"You will not." I was surprised by the snap to my voice, even though I knew she was messing with me.

She didn't argue. Instead, she softened her voice. "You deserve a great guy. A nice guy. A *hot* guy. You deserve every orgasm he can give you."

"Marina!"

"What? You do. You might look at vaginas all day, but I bet yours has cobwebs on it."

I was *not* answering that one.

"Boyd Wolf is cocky. Sure of himself," I countered.

"So? That makes him good in bed."

I sighed, took a deep breath. "He's definitely a player. Listen, I'm here. I have to go."

"Have fun. Don't do anything I wouldn't do. Actually, forget that. Do everything I wouldn't do and then some."

She ended the call as I rolled my eyes. I leaned forward and looked up at the arch. *Wolf Ranch.* I had no idea what I was doing, driving all the way out here. Boyd Wolf was fine. Marina was right. I'd been wrong about how seriously he'd been injured. There was no other explanation. Yet...

Fine, I wanted to see him again, to believe he really was healed. Or not hurt. He couldn't have healed if he hadn't really been hurt. Gah!

I dropped my forehead to the top of the steering wheel. I was fooling myself if it was only my need for answers that had me idling in front of his ranch. I was interested in knowing more about Boyd than as a doctor. I wanted to know why his abs were like a washboard. Why his skin was hot and smooth. If the chest hair I'd felt disappeared beneath the waistband of his jeans.

If his cocky attitude meant he was cocky in bed. If he'd be bossy and stern...

Yeah, I was totally screwed.

5

UDREY

I'D MADE it all the way down the long drive and to the main house but hadn't gotten out of the car. My pep talk had gotten me this far but had fizzled out just shy of the front door. I sat in my idling car when a rap sounded on my window.

I shrieked a little and nearly wrenched my neck looking out at the... wow. Those were some broad shoulders under that cowboy hat. It was another *very* good-looking cowboy. He didn't look happy. Where the hell had he come from? I'd been staring at the house—a full on farmhouse of epic proportions—but not too focused to have missed someone of his size approaching.

I quickly shut off the car and opened my door. The man stepped back, still frowning. He resembled Boyd, except a little older, and everywhere Boyd radiated happy go lucky, this guy radiated grumpy. I took a guess at him being an older brother.

"Hi! I'm Dr. Ames." I reached back into the car, fumbled with my purse and medical kit and pulled them out, spun back around to face the guy, then stuck out my hand. Yeah, I was flustered. "I'm here to check in on Boyd."

He looked down at his own hands, dusting them on his jeans, then held them up. "I'm not fit to shake," he said, although I suspected he just didn't want to touch me. Which was stupid, and I was certainly reading way too much into it. "You're... what did you say? A *doctor*? Why would you need to come all the way out here to check on Boyd?"

I didn't know why, but his skepticism or confusion offended me. I frowned, stared him down, then squared my shoulders. "Yes. I attended Boyd when he was injured at the rodeo the other night. He left the hospital without completing the proper discharge papers."

Shock and disbelief flickered over the man's face, then his scowl deepened. "I see. I'm sorry, my little brother does have a habit of operating outside the rules."

Okay. It seemed there was a little family tension here. I gave a bland shrug to make light of it all. "It's fine. I just wanted to check on his wound. Is he here?"

I looked away from the gorgeous grumpy guy. The long dirt drive where I'd parked sloped down to a giant barn, a stable and corral. In front of me stood a large ranch house with plenty of windows and a wrap-around porch. A beautiful place to raise a huge family. Lots of rooms, lots of places for kids to run and play while the parents sat in rocking chairs on the front porch and watched. A pang of envy filled me. I couldn't imagine growing up in a place as idyllic as this, and I was... jealous.

I'd been raised by a single mom with depression. It

hadn't been a Norman Rockwell painting like this place probably was.

To the left, a long two-story building stood with a similar porch on the ground floor and a balcony running all along the top floor. Doors opened to the top balcony, almost like the ranch version of a dorm or apartment building. A bunkhouse, perhaps? How many people lived and worked here? On a piece of land this size, I assumed a fair amount.

"I'm right here, Doc."

A deep voice had me spinning on my heel in the direction of the road that led to the barn. Boyd came jogging up in a pair of ripped jeans and fitted t-shirt in hunter green, a few flecks of straw on the shoulder. There wasn't a hint of effort in his gait as if he was injured. The relaxed smile on his face didn't indicate pain or discomfort. The snug shirt couldn't hide any kind of bandage.

He tugged off a pair of work gloves as he came up, his smile as wide and charming as I remembered it. For one moment, I forgot everything under the glare of that magnetic white-toothed grin. Heat blossomed between my legs, my nipples tightened in my bra. *This* feeling was why I was standing here, why I'd driven all this way. I felt like *I'd* been hit by a charging bull, and I'd never, ever felt like this before.

Not over a man. Not over a man I didn't even know. Gah.

But then reality came crashing back.

What in the hell was happening? How was it possible?

I'd have sworn on a stack of Bibles this man had been a bloody mess just two days ago. Now it looked like he'd been throwing hay bales out in the barn. No way could a guy with a sucking chest wound be able to twist his body, let alone throw hay.

As if he was suddenly reminded of his injury, he sagged

a bit, bracing his ribs with his forearm with one hand, then took off his hat with the other. His light hair was damp with sweat and had a crease from his hat. I wanted to ruffle it with my fingers.

"Awful nice of you to come check up on me."

Again, that devastating grin.

Again, the ruined panties.

"What the hell happened to you?" Boyd's brother demanded.

"Doc, this is Rob, my brother."

I nodded as a way of hello. I couldn't tell if Rob was bothered by my presence or bothered by Boyd or just all around a cranky person, but I didn't want to find out.

"You didn't answer my question. What happened?" Was that a growl in Rob's voice?

Boyd rolled his eyes. "Nothing."

Boyd grabbed my wrist and tugged me away from Rob and back in the direction he'd come. I had to practically run to keep up with his long gait. The sun was warm, and my shirt began to cling to me. I glanced back at Rob who stood where we'd left him by my car, watching us.

"Where are we going?" I asked, trying to catch my breath.

"Somewhere alone." He slowed down and glanced down at me. His gaze held heat. Promise. Need. All of it was potent and made me catch my breath in a way a dash across the property ever could.

Somewhere alone. My body was thinking that was an incredibly good idea. My mind... not so much.

———

BOYD

. . .

I DIDN'T SHUT the barn door behind us, although I wanted to lock it up tight to keep Audrey in… and everyone else out. My wolf howled with enthusiasm that she was here with me. She'd shown up, just as I'd assumed, but it had taken two fucking days. I'd rubbed one out in the shower morning and night, my dick getting hard just thinking about her. The curve of her cheek, the lush swell of her tits, the roundness of her hips, the berry color of her lips. The thought of those lips trying to wrap around every inch of me. I was big, and she was a little thing and would have a hard time. At first.

Fuck, my dick was punching against the zipper of my jeans, and all I wanted to do was push her up against the wall, tug down her pants and drive into her. Or, I could bend her over a saddle stand and take her from behind, spank her ass for making me wait two days to see her again. To breathe in that sweet scent.

That was what had pulled me from my chores. Peaches. I knew she was here the second I breathed her in, even from afar. I'd know her anywhere by that alone. And then she'd been talking to Rob. The fucker had not been happy to see her. Hell, he wasn't happy to see anyone. As alpha, he was protective of our land, of our way of life. Any outsider, no matter how fucking gorgeous or perfect for my wolf, would get a cold shoulder. Plus, he kept his distance from all females—shifter or human. He wouldn't say why, but I suspected he might be getting a trace of moon madness. It could overcome male wolves—particularly alphas—when they haven't mated by a certain age. Turned them wild—feral. If it went on too long, the shifter could lose his humanity altogether.

"Um… what are we doing in here?"

Her voice was soft and gentle, although there was an underlying hint of command to it. It was the same tone she'd used with me at the arena, one that said she wasn't amused. She might be a foot shorter, but somehow, she seemed to look down her nose at me. If I hadn't known she was a doctor, I'd think her a stern librarian, with those fuck-me glasses and all.

"Getting you away from my brother. He's somewhat of an asshole."

She glanced over her shoulder toward the open doorway, which practically glowed from the bright sunshine. We stood in the darkened interior, the air cooler here. I'd spent the morning tossing hay bales into the loft with the other pack members, who'd made themselves scarce now. Wolf Ranch was huge, over ten thousand acres. Plenty for a pack of shifters to roam without veering onto someone else's land. The pack totaled about forty members. Ten lived on the ranch. All males. All unmated. Other mated wolves lived nearby in the hills, preferring an even more remote location or their own space because they had a family. Pups.

It was only a matter of time before all of us would succumb to the urge to mate, where the need overrode anything else. I'd felt hints of mine, the need to find The One growing stronger. It was when that urge wasn't obeyed —when someone held out for The One but didn't find her and didn't take another instead—that there was trouble with moon madness. Lucky for me, I met Audrey, and I knew she was it. My mate. My wolf knew, all but pushed me to claim her here and now.

But she wasn't a shifter. She was human. She didn't know we even existed let alone want to *mate* with a wolf.

I was totally fucked. The way she was looking up at me,

expectant and filled with a degree of annoyance, was hot as hell. Everything she did turned me on. I couldn't miss the way her tits rose and fell as she breathed. The pulse point in her neck throbbed with her life blood at the spot I wanted to sink my teeth into as I fucked her hard. Made her mine.

Fuck!

"I didn't tell him about the accident in the arena," I explained. "I didn't want him to worry—you know?" More like, I didn't want him to know how I'd fucked things up by getting myself taken to a hospital. Having my healing witnessed by Audrey. I'd recovered completely by the time I'd driven to the ranch, grabbed a shower and threw out my bloodied clothes.

I aimed my most charming smile at her. "He already thinks I'm wasting my life in the rodeo."

I give her a wink, stepping into her personal space.

She responded to my nearness, some of her disapproval dropping away and sympathy creeping in. "Yes, I did pick up on some of that."

I knew she was a smart one.

I give her a lazy shrug. "I'm the black sheep of the family."

I was the third Wolf son. Rob was the alpha and Colton was the beta. He was two years older than me and had enlisted fresh out of high school. He was off saving the fucking world as a Green Beret, but he knew his place, knew he'd have to return to the ranch eventually, especially after the urge to mate hit. Rob and Colton were the heir and the spare. I was the third wheel. I would never hold rank in the pack. I'd known that forever. And when our parents had been killed… I'd hidden the pain with a who-gave-a-fuck attitude. The second I graduated, I'd also left the ranch, made my own way. Became the champ on the back of a bull.

My last name might be over the archway at the entrance to the ranch, but I wasn't needed here. I was just the fuck up. I'd proven that again coming back. Audrey wasn't here to get in my pants. She'd made that clear as fucking day. She was here because she was smart. A doctor. She questioned. She wanted to know the truth.

I couldn't tell her the truth. It would destroy the pack. While I didn't feel like I belonged, I'd do nothing to hurt the Wolf pack. Nothing. So while I needed to push Audrey away, to get her back in her little car and on the road back to Cooper Valley, she wasn't going to go without answers.

Answers I couldn't give.

There was only one way I could think of to keep from telling her the truth.

Distraction.

It was time to lay on the Wolf charm because one way to make a woman forget that she'd encountered a quick-healing wolf was to make her forget her own name.

I might be a fuck up in some things, but I certainly knew how to do that particular trick. My wolf? He thought that was a mighty fine idea.

I grinned and her blue eyes widened. "Besides, I wanted you all to myself. What brings you here? Couldn't resist Boyd Wolf, darlin'?"

She frowned. "I came to see to your injuries, just like I said."

I tucked my forearm against my side, like I was covering the wound. "Nah, I told you, I'm fine." I inched closer. "I'll let you in on a little secret." I was using my best bedroom voice. "I'm not the kinda guy who submits for examinations. In fact—" I let my hands settle lightly on her waist. "I prefer to be the one in charge." I dropped my head, bringing our foreheads close. "Doing the examining, I mean."

Her mouth fell open. She quickly shut it, licked her lips. The way her little pink tongue flicked out... fuck. This was supposed to get her distracted, not make my balls tighten and turn blue.

She lifted her hand as if to touch the spot where the horn had pierced but stopped just in time. I took hold of her fingers, pulled them to my chest. She gasped.

I growled, and she whipped her head up to mine at the sound.

"I... um." She tried to tug her hand free, but I wasn't letting go.

When she stopped trying to pull away, I loosened my hold but moved her hand over my chest so her fingertips could graze the line of my pectoral muscle. Goosebumps rose, my cock swelled. My wolf howled.

She was watching her fingers, and I couldn't miss, even in the dim light since I had excellent vision, that her pupils were dilated. That thrum at her neck... it had picked up.

I inhaled deeply, breathing in that peach scent. And more. "You're sweet everywhere, aren't you, darlin'?"

Yeah, her pussy was going to be so fucking sweet. Sticky sweet because she was wet. I didn't have to slip my hand into her panties to know for sure. This close, with only the earthy scents of the barn as a distraction, I couldn't miss her arousal.

"I... I came to—"

"You haven't come yet, Audrey," I murmured, cutting her off. Keeping her hand, I walked forward a step, forcing her to retreat. I turned, so we were facing the opposite direction, then walked her so her back was pressed against the side of the barn. "But you will."

"Um."

That was all she said before I lowered my head and

kissed her. A gentle brushing, soft, as if to learn the feel of those soft pillows of flesh. I kissed one corner, her mouth open as she began to pant, then the other. I ran my hand down over her hair, silky soft, then gripped the thick strands at the nape of her neck and tugged. Not too hard, but she gasped, and her eyes opened wide. But blurry.

I didn't say anything, just kissed her again. This time, she knew I was in control. My tongue swept across her lip, then delved deep, finding hers. Her free hand went to my biceps, held on.

She tasted sweet, perfect. Leaning forward, I pressed into her. Her soft tits plumped against my chest, and my dick nestled against her belly. My back bent to reach her, our height difference so great.

I growled, grabbed her hips and lifted her up, then pressed her back into the wall again now that our mouths were lined up. Her dangling legs came up and around, behind me, not long enough to hook her feet together, so her heels hooked against my lower back. Her pussy, fuck... her pussy was pressed right against my length now, and I felt her heat through both of our jeans. My hips jerked into her, and she moaned.

I took advantage and nibbled along her jaw, down the line of her neck. She angled her chin up, offering me access. Her sharp little nails dug into my shoulders. Fuck, she was a little wildcat.

I lifted my head enough to take her in. Wet, swollen lips, flushed cheeks, hazy gaze, ragged breath. Her hair was mussed from my hand, and her glasses were crooked. *Fuck, yes.*

Except, for the first time in my life, I experienced a stab of guilt at seducing her so quickly. My wolf was down—oh boy, was he down, but there was something behind it all.

Maybe because I knew this was so much more than the figurative and literal roll in the hay. This female was my mate—even though it made no logical sense. I hadn't dared even think that one word... mate. I'd said from the first time I saw her that she was mine, but mate? That word was powerful.

Too fucking powerful because she was human and didn't belong here or in the pack. Yet I couldn't deny the rightness of kissing her. Of touching her. Having her press against me, hearing the sweet sounds of her pleasure that me and my wolf brought out. In the past, I'd felt cocky knowing I could get a woman all hot and bothered. With Audrey, it was different. Hot as fucking hell, but reverent somehow. As if the sounds she made were precious, were just for me.

And instead of asking her on a date and taking my time to get to know her, I had her pushed against the barn wall, drunk on pheromones. I was everything I didn't want to be. This wasn't happy-go-lucky wham bam thank you, ma'am. This was so much more.

I hated myself in this moment because while it was special, I had no other choice. I couldn't very well lift my shirt and show her there wasn't even a mark where that bull's horn went through my side. I had to be the asshole who seduced her for a reason, and it wasn't only because she was mine and I wanted to hear every desperate sound she made, to feel the prick of her nails, the catch to her breath. No, it was because I had to make her forget all about the fact that I was a fucking shifter and she was human and we'd never be right, no matter how much my wolf said so.

Because of all that bullshit and not because I needed to with every cell in my body, I went back to kissing the hell out of her. Making her forget all about that unfortunate incident. I could get her off and get her back in her car in under a minute.

I lifted my head. She was my mate. I couldn't be a dick. She might not be able to be mine and I might not be able to claim her, but I could show her what it could be like between us. I wouldn't fake anything. Hell, I'd give it my all, so she'd come like never before. If this was it, then I wanted it to be as special as I could make it, so I could remember. Could make it the top of my spank bank file for the rest of my life. This was perfection, and I had to savor every second.

My tongue swept between her lips, danced against hers. My palms slid down to cup her ass. I squeezed and kneaded those perfect globes as I took my fill of her mouth.

I had to scratch that. I probably would never get my fill. Because tasting her was like an arrival.

The achievement I'd been searching for without knowing it all these years. My wolf nudged me, snarled, agreeing with me not to be a dick and do this right. I couldn't take from her for a reason.

I had to give.

6

Boyd

"You feel so fucking good, Doc," I murmured against her ear when I finally broke the kiss. "You feel feverish." I nipped her earlobe. "Hot all over. What other symptoms you got? Dampness between your legs?" I ground my hardened dick against the apex of her thighs once again.

"Jesus, Boyd." Her head fell back against the wooden boards. She sounded breathless.

I wanted to roll on a condom and sink into that delicious heat, but I wasn't going to. For one thing, I was supposed to be injured. For another, this wasn't for my pleasure—it was for hers.

I eased her away from the wall, so her feet came down, then worked the button on her jeans. "I'm going to need to give you a thorough examination, Doctor." I inched her zipper lower at the same time I nibbled along the side of her neck.

"Oh...um... wow." Fuck, I loved that breathy quality of her voice. "I'm supposed to be checking on you."

I grinned, then nipped at the juncture of her neck and shoulder. The spot where I wanted to bite and mark her as mine. No. *No!*

"You take care of everyone. It's time someone takes care of you."

She was still thinking too much, so I slid my hand inside her opened jeans, then over the lacy edge of her panties. Silk and lace. Fuck, I wanted to see them, but kept on my task, which was far from a hardship. Sure, I wanted her to forget about my injury, but I wanted to see her come. Wanted to see her face as she found her peak on my fingers. Heard the sounds of her release. I needed it more than I wanted to come. Yes, she was my mate. No fucking question if I didn't give a shit if my balls turned blue and fell off as long as my girl got off.

I brushed my fingers lightly over her folds with no barrier but the thin fabric of her panties. She was hot and the silk wet.

Her pussy clenched, breath stuttered. Her scent was stronger now, her body temperature rising, sweat blooming on her skin, her pussy all but coating her panties in her sweet-scented juices.

I made a circle over her clit. "I'd like to pay you back, Doctor." I swallowed her gasp with a kiss, not able to resist her mouth. I could finger fuck her, find that little g-spot and rub it and stroke that clit until she screamed and creamed. But no. She'd get more from me, and I'd remember everything about this moment.

I could hear birds chirping outside the barn, the rustle of the wind. No one was around. I'd hear them coming a long way off. Audrey was mine. Every pant. Every moan. Every clench of her pussy.

"For the care you gave me when I was hurt," I added. I tucked one finger under the gusset of her panties and dragged it through her juices. I groaned. My wolf growled. That nectar was all for me. She was ready for my cock, to be marked, mated. Made mine.

"Th-that's not really necessary." Her hips bucked as I slowly circled her entrance, dipped inside. Her pussy muscles clenched the tip of my finger. She was tight. Hot. Wet. She'd probably strangle my dick if I got in her.

"Want me to stop?"

She shook her head. "No. Oh, don't stop."

I grinned, licked her sweaty skin.

"Maybe I should," I replied, stilling my finger.

"Boyd," she practically begged.

"Are you a good girl, Audrey?"

She opened her eyes, blinked up at me slowly as if she was trying to clear her head. "Always."

Yeah, I believed that.

"I think there's a bad girl in you. I think when you get going, you're *very* naughty."

"I—"

"You're in the barn with me, my finger inside you." With that, I slid that one digit in slowly, but nice and deep. She moaned, gripped my arms, clenched down hard.

"Good girls don't get fingerfucked up against a wall," I said against her ear. My wolf could hear the way her heartbeat accelerated, and I couldn't miss the way her pussy gushed all over my hand. Yeah, Audrey liked to get dirty.

"Good girls don't get their pussies licked." I kissed down her neck, across her collarbone. I bit the fabric of her shirt over her nipple. Then I dropped to my knees and tugged her pants and panties down to her thighs.

She mewled, her feet shifting with the sudden change. Her pussy was neatly trimmed. Sweet. Beautiful. The scent of her nectar sent my blood zinging, and this close, it made my mouth water. I leaned in and kissed it softly once, then licked into her folds.

My hat was in the way, so I took it off, set it on the ground beside me.

And then I couldn't hold back. I wrestled her pants lower, so I could pry her thighs wide. I lifted one and delved my tongue everywhere—between her folds, around her clit, inside her swollen entrance. She was as fucking sweet as I thought. As it coated my lips, my chin... I knew I'd know this scent anywhere. I was marked. Everyone on the ranch would know exactly where I'd been, and that made my wolf puff up with pride and made me one possessive fucker.

"Oh!" Her slender fingers wove into my hair at first—I thought—to steady herself, then urging me on, pulling my face into her juicy flesh. I licked and teased, even let my teeth graze her sensitive nubbin of pleasure. That made her tug, made it hurt so good.

Her thigh pressed against my ear, trembling. Her stomach shuddered on her breaths, and the sounds she made—fuck! My dick was harder than stone listening to those little frantic breaths and cries. Pre-cum spurted from the throbbing tip and stained my boxers and jeans. It would definitely leave a mark.

I screwed one finger into her and pumped it while I sucked her clit. Her standing leg buckled, but I wouldn't let her fall. I held her up, pinned between my mouth and the barn wall.

"Boyd. *Ohmygod—Boyd*."

I fucking loved the sound of my name on her lips, especially with that desperate tremor to her voice, her taste on my tongue, her inner walls rippling around my thick finger.

I worked a second into her tight channel and curled both of them to stroke her inner wall, seeking her g-spot. The moment I found it, she gave a strangled cry. The tissue raised and stiffened under my fingers. I couldn't help but grin against that perfect center of sweet flesh knowing she was so responsive for me. That I was right. She was a bad, bad girl.

She seemed almost surprised by the pleasure I could pull from her, and that meant one thing. She'd never been like this for anyone else. She was bad. And mine.

I went for a slow build, first caressing her g-spot, then rubbing it as I finger-fucked her until she came. Hard.

She tore at my hair. "Boyd! Holy—ohmygod." Her voice rose in pitch. "Oh my God!"

She came, her hips snapping, her channel putting the squeeze on my fingers as she moaned and gasped out her release. I couldn't cover her mouth or stifle her sounds, not that I wanted to miss one bit of it. It was all for me. My sweet reward. I slowed my thrusts, then stroked her inner wall, until she sagged back, limp.

Slipping my fingers from her, I licked them as I looked up at her. Her glasses were crooked, her hair was snagged in spots on the rough wood of the wall. "You're gorgeous when you're a good girl, but when you're bad—*fuck*, Doc."

7

Audrey

I HEARD Boyd's words but was slow to process. I opened my eyes, looked down at him, still on his knees before me, licking his finger. The finger that had just been inside me and given me the best orgasm of my life. Oh. My. God.

"Yeah, everything seems to be in working order, Doc," Boyd murmured, his voice deeper than it had been when we started.

Oh God. What just happened?

You just came all over his face. My arousal actually coated his chin, some satisfied part of myself said. Maybe it was my body. My poor, neglected body. I'd been primed from years of withdrawal.

I pushed my glasses up on my nose, blinking to get the stars out of them. My mouth was swollen from his kisses, my neck tingled from beard burn. And my pussy... My body buzzed, warmth and heat still pulsing through in a slow, satisfied rhythm.

Boyd straightened and pulled my panties up, then my pants, then zipped and buttoned them as if he hadn't just gotten in them and gotten me off faster than a rocket on a ten second countdown. I'd never had a man dress me before, and somehow, it felt almost more intimate than what he'd just done. As if this was something special.

"Um... wow. Whoa."

Great. Real articulate, Audrey.

I dragged my fingers through my hair to straighten the mess. I was sure I looked exactly like a woman who'd just had a roll in the hay. "Do you do that with every woman who shows up at the ranch?"

I cursed myself for sounding so breathless.

His eyes narrowed. "No way. Not at all."

Except he looked guilty, like he definitely *did* do this with every woman who showed up.

Okay, well, I had no regrets. I wasn't going to slut-shame myself for indulging in the sexiest cowboy alive. I didn't want to be a notch on his belt, but I had just come so hard, I was still seeing stars. My body had definitely deserved some attention, and this bull rider certainly knew his stuff. Holy shit, did he. Marina had said go for it, and I sure as hell had.

But he didn't fit the picture I planned for my future. The devoted husband. Did the guy who gave me babies talk dirty and finger fuck me up against the side of the barn? This wasn't how it was supposed to be, was it? I *was* a good girl and imagined a wild romp in bed. Maybe the lights would stay on. Maybe a few unusual positions for it to be fun and different. But this?

Wow.

This just proved that Boyd was obviously after one thing: another conquest. We'd barely talked, and he had my jeans and panties around my thighs. And while I enjoyed—okay, I way more than enjoyed—that sexy interlude, I couldn't take this further. Who was I kidding? He probably wouldn't want to either.

I wasn't judging him or his sexual proclivities, but I was the type who preferred sex in a committed relationship. To me, it was about deepening intimacy, exchanging love. A fun time in the barn wasn't any of those things. After my mother not even knowing who my dad was, I wasn't keen on one-night stands. I wanted what I'd never had growing up. A family. So yeah, if I stayed, I'd get addicted to those fingers and tongue. If he got his dick out, I'd probably be ruined forever.

I needed to get the hell out of here before this thing got any more out of hand.

Boyd leaned against the side of the barn and adjusted the bulge in his jeans. The huge bulge that ran down the inside of his thigh. Holy shit, all *that* was his dick?

I wanted to see it. All those inches. Touch it, feel the heat of it, the hardness. I doubted my fingers would get around it. My satisfied pussy clenched at the thought of that thing fitting in me.

No!

I was never going to find out how it would stretch me open, make me feel so full.

And a thing of that size stuck inside his well-worn jeans? A pang of guilt ran through me at leaving him blue-balled, but hey. I wasn't the one to initiate this thing.

"So, Doc. You ready to take me up on that tour of the area?" He gave me that cocky, crooked smile. The one that got women out of their panties. Including me. "There are so many beautiful places to see in Cooper Valley."

I bent down to pick up my keys, which must've fallen from my pocket during our romp. "Thank you, Boyd." I glanced up at him, realized his dick was right at my eye level and stood up abruptly. "I, ah, appreciate the offer, but like I said before, I don't have much time off. In fact, I need to get back to work right now." I started backing toward the open barn door. "Because this was just hospital business, you know."

He followed me, staying in the circle of my personal space, making me so damn susceptible to his charm. "Business," he murmured mockingly. "Uh huh."

"Yes. I came to check on—"

"I know." He waved away my focus from his abdomen—the area of his wound. "But now you know I'm fine. And I know you're pretty magnificent, yourself. Tasty, too."

Oh, that sexy cowboy swagger. That dirty mouth.

Yeah, I'd do him again. And that made me everything he said. I was a bad girl. No good girl would think of doing what we'd just done.

Eek.

And that was why I needed to run the hell away from Wolf Ranch as fast as I could.

Boyd Wolf was temptation simmering in a gorgeous cowboy package. And I needed to remove myself from his influence before I tugged down his jeans and had my way with *him*.

I stumbled through the open barn door and then turned, walking swiftly toward my car.

"You sure, Doctor Ames?" he called from behind me. "I'll be around for a few more days, at least."

I stopped and turned, my professional instincts

returning. "You can't return to work until you've had a complete physical. I explicitly told your bosses that."

A flicker of annoyance crossed his face, which irritated the hell out of me. This guy was *way* too alpha male. And everyone knew, they made the very worst patients of all.

"Looks like you were the one who got the physical," he countered.

I blushed so hotly, it was possible I would burst into flames. He didn't just say that. The cocky little shit!

I spared us both the goodbyes. Leaving swiftly was far more important than pleasantries that being a good girl would have had me said. I slid into my seat and slammed the door, jamming the key in the ignition.

Dammit! I dropped the keyring onto the floorboard. I leaned over to pick it up, frustration making my eyes burn with unshed tears. I knew Boyd still stood there watching, even though I refused to look. His magnetic field pulled women in from miles around. I'd probably feel it the entire drive down the road.

I started the car up and threw it in reverse, backing up way faster than I usually did. Boyd lifted his hand in a wave. I tried not to look, but he got me. Those green eyes trained straight through the rearview mirror, pinning me with a stare. For once, the cocky smile wasn't present. He almost appeared... dismayed.

But that didn't make sense. Boyd Wolf packed enough ego to last him a lifetime. He surely wouldn't mourn one lost opportunity with a short, bespectacled doctor who could lose fifteen pounds and had zero game. Maybe it was because he hadn't gotten off, that I was leaving before he had a happy ending of his own.

Only because the sun was in my eyes, I watched him in my mirror as I drove away.

Boyd never moved. He just stood there, staring at the back of my car like he'd lost his best friend.

I was sure I imagined that last part. No bad boy like him gave that notch on his bedpost a second glance.

Totally sure.

8

Boyd

Fuck. I couldn't have screwed things up any worse.

No, that wasn't true. I kept Audrey from getting a look at my wound, and I made her come. That had to mean something.

Why, then, did I feel this nagging heaviness about the way things went down? Why was my wolf moping, nudging me to go after her?

I had no idea how long I stood there, but it was enough time for Rob to stalk up from the corral without me noticing.

"You gonna tell me what all this is about?" he rumbled. I was in trouble if I could let a two-hundred plus pound shifter sneak up on me.

I glared at the dust that had kicked up behind Audrey's car at the end of our long dirt drive.

"Boyd?" he prompted. "What the fuck happened?"

I pulled my gloves out of my pocket and put them on, turning to stalk back to the barn. My dick was hurting, my balls ached to be emptied. I'd take care of it later in the shower, but I had to bleed off the excess energy somehow. Shifting and going for a run would work, but there were chores to be done. Unsaid ranch rules were chores first, run after.

"I asked you a question." Rob infused alpha command into his voice as he caught my shoulder, and I went still, my body responding instinctively to the pack leader. I didn't look at him, though. I couldn't.

He wasn't just my alpha. He wasn't just my brother. He'd played the role of my father... hell, both parents, after they'd been killed when I was twelve. It had been my fault he'd been thrust into the role of alpha and parent in the blink of an eye. Mom and Dad had headed into Cooper Valley for me. While Rob and Colton had already started to shift by the time they were my age, they'd called me defective. Two and four years older, they left me behind when they went off and roamed the property. I'd been jealous, hurt and didn't think myself much of a shifter.

You're not a shifter if you can't shift, they'd taunted.

Instead of embracing the pack life, I'd pretended I was completely human. I'd wanted to go to the county fair and meet my school friends. Friends who couldn't shift, like me. I'd spent the day there, with the plan that my parents would pick me up at ten by the entrance. I'd dared my friend to have a third corndog and go on the Tilt-A-Whirl without hurling. There'd been five dollars in it, and I'd only realized what time it was when thunder clapped overhead. I'd left Bobby Sweetin to puke his guts out minus the five dollars.

I'd been seventeen minutes late.

Seventeen minutes where we could have been through

the canyon before the rock slide, before our car had been knocked off the road and partially crushed. I'd survived without a scratch. My parents? The state patrol said they'd been killed in an instant.

They might not have suffered, but I did. Every fucking day. If I hadn't been such a little shit and kept them waiting, Rob wouldn't have been forced to skip college to take care of the pack and two little brothers.

It had been my fault, and I knew it. I was the family fuck-up. Turned out, I wasn't defective because I couldn't shift—I'd survived the accident because I'd shifted and been able to get out of the mangled truck in my new wolf form. Four paws had gotten me up the wet bank. I was defective because I'd destroyed the Wolf pack with one stupid middle-school prank.

I'd been wild and reckless after that and hadn't stopped. I might not be an alpha of a pack, but I was king of the rodeo. I was invincible, literally. I had nothing to fear on the back of a bull. I might get hurt, but not for long.

Except this time, I had a lot to worry about. I might have recovered fast, but I'd been distracted, just like at the county fair. This time, it was by Abe's hand on Audrey's shoulder. That bit of jealousy could destroy the pack all over again. Audrey suspected. While I had no problem getting her off for the rest of her life to distract her, I didn't think that was going to work. She wasn't a ditzy buckle bunny out for a good time. Audrey Ames was all brains... and had one sweet, addictive pussy.

"Talk. *Now*." More alpha command.

I sighed, prepared myself for his anger and disappointment and glanced at him over my shoulder. "I got gored at the last rodeo, and she was the arena doc." I didn't elaborate on why I got gored in the first place, only highlighting how stupid I'd been. He wouldn't approve of mating a human. He wouldn't believe I had the urge to mark her as mine.

His eyebrows went up, but he didn't show much emotion. He never did. I knew never to play poker with the fucker. "Seriously, Boyd? How did that happen?"

I didn't answer because I'd already decided I wasn't telling him that Audrey was mine. Not yet, anyway. Not until I'd explored it further.

I wasn't *that* stupid.

I wanted more with her. Not that what we just did in the barn didn't count as a whole fucking lot.

"Let me guess—you were more focused on getting some pussy than you were on staying on your bull?" The sound of disgust in Rob's voice raised my hackles, but it was the fact that he was right that really burned me.

It also made me want to punch him in the fucking throat. Because Audrey was *not* some pussy. She was so much more. I wanted to tell him off for disrespecting her like that, but I couldn't.

I turned to face him head on, a snarl on my lip. "I'm taking care of the problem, so you can fuck off."

And that was how I ended up with my hat flying off and me landing ass first in the dirt with my nose bleeding. His fist came up out of nowhere. I might have killer reflexes to keep my ass on the back of a bull, but Rob had alpha reflexes and a whole fuckton of command to go with it.

No one challenged an alpha wolf. Especially not when there was family history. It was definitely broken, and my nose hurt like a bitch. I sniffed, wiped the dripping blood with the back of my hand and picked up Audrey's scent. My fingers were covered with it from fingering her. My wolf snapped and snarled, not caring I'd been laid out, but that

Rob was getting in the way of me being with Audrey. Still, I couldn't explain because all he'd do was shut me down not with his fist this time, but an alpha command to stay the fuck away from her.

I stayed down and showed my throat to signify my surrender to his pack position.

Rob folded his arms over his chest and glared down at me. "The fact that you're being an asshole tells me we have a real problem here. I'm going to fill in the blanks, so correct me if I'm wrong. You got hurt at an event, and she treated you, discovered you healed fucking fast and was curious. Something like that?"

I gave him one quick nod.

"How much does that doctor know and what are you going to do about it?"

I rolled to my side and stood, brushed the dirt off my ass, ignoring the blood as I set the break. Pack justice was often physical because there was no real harm. My nose would heal within the hour. My perpetually wounded pride and neverending guilt? I was still waiting for that to fix.

"She rode with me in the ambulance to the hospital—"

"Ambulance? What the fuck did you do to yourself?"

I didn't answer that, just finished my explanation. "—then she saw me walk out not long after. I have it under control."

One of his dark brows winged up in a look that screamed *yeah right*. "How exactly? By getting into her pants and getting her off? Don't think I can't smell her scent all over you. Did your magic dick solve this colossal fuck-up?"

Yeah, that stung. He'd hit the bullseye with his words and made my plan sound like the dumbest idea ever. I shrugged. "Kept her from examining me, and she's off the ranch." It sounded lame even to my own ears.

Rob looked down the drive where she'd disappeared. His next order took me by surprise. "That doctor is too smart to fall for your shenanigans. You might have needed to hide out here for a few days to miraculously heal, but you're not leaving town until we know this situation has been contained. You need to stay on her."

"What?" I asked.

He pursed his lips and set his hands on his hips. "Make yourself her new best friend until she's convinced you're the most ordinary human male in the county."

I preferred she believe I was extraordinary in a few areas, but I didn't bother arguing that point with Rob. Instead of him ordering me to never see her again like I'd expected, he told me to do the exact fucking opposite.

He wanted me to be her best friend. Well, that wasn't fucking happening. Best friends didn't finger fuck or get eaten out. But see her again and maybe again and again? My wolf practically howled, and I was getting hard at the thought of tasting her. And more.

But how could I be with her and not claim her completely? I couldn't just fuck her and forget her as Rob was insinuating. Sure, that was my MO since I lost my virginity in Mary Sanchez's basement in twelfth grade. Maybe this idea was bad. Really bad. I wanted her for my mate. For forever. Rob wanted it temporary and until any possible thought of the existence of shifters was forgotten.

He wouldn't want me to claim her. Hell, no. If he had any idea of my need to mate her, he'd punch me in the face again and set one of the ranch hands on her to watch her for a while.

No fucking way.

So I'd do what he said and try to figure out how to make

her mine and somehow keep the fact I was a shifter a total secret at the same time.

I nodded and stuck my hat back on my head. "Done."

My wolf was happy as fuck. I'd finish my chores, get cleaned up and head into town. Track down Audrey and become her best friend—who would soon be fucking her until her headboard broke. I couldn't have asked for a more appealing assignment and potentially the biggest mistake of my life.

I was a risktaker, and this was one fucking huge risk. This wasn't riding an angry bull. This was making my wolf happy.

There was no fucking way I was going to walk away when this task was over. I wasn't going back to the rodeo and riding bulls. Not unless my sweet doctor came with me.

I wasn't going anywhere without Audrey.

She was mine and mine alone.

I just had to make sure she got on board with that plan, too.

9

Audrey

"That's it, I can see your baby's head," I coaxed my patient. Alana had been in labor for twenty-three hours and was definitely getting tired.

"You're almost there, Mama," Becky, the nurse said, rubbing her shoulder. "Think how amazing it will feel to hold your sweet baby in your arms."

Alana whimpered and nodded, sweat beading on her forehead. She'd wanted an all-natural birth, and I always honored my patient's wishes unless I deemed it completely medically necessary to intervene. So when labor stalled, I had Becky walk her up and down the hallway rather than give her a shot of Pitocin to get things going again. It worked. The weight of the baby's head on her cervix caused it to dilate, and labor picked back up. Now she was just a few more pushes from the finish line.

"Another push when you feel the urge. No, wait for the

urge," I coached. The monitors showed another contraction, and Alana pushed. "That's it." A tiny dark-haired head slid out, and I cradled it in my gloved hands.

"Oh my God!" Alana's husband gulped, tears in his voice. He stood by her side holding her hand. "The head is out, angel."

Alana gave a sob. Her body pushed again, and one shoulder slid out, then another.

"You're there!" I told her. On the next push, the slippery bundle slid into my hands. "You did it! It's a girl."

"A girl! Oh my God, we have a girl!" Alana wept, as I set the newborn on her chest. Becky covered her with a warm blanket and rubbed her back. Her husband wept.

Becky wept.

I blinked back the film of tears from my eyes and gave a watery laugh.

This moment was why I'd chosen to be an ObGyn. Even as grounded in science as I was and always have been, I was always moved by the miracle of birth. Nature at its most beautiful. Most joyful. It didn't mean every situation was happy, and I didn't encounter my share of sad tears, too. For the most part, it was an upbeat profession.

I helped Alana with the afterbirth, then waited to cut the cord. Alana was one of those all-natural-kind-of women who knitted their own baby caps before birth and had strong opinions about how much medical intervention they wanted. She'd read that her baby needed its cord blood, and it was better to delay the cutting. I saw no harm in delaying. Instead of untethering the baby and giving her to Becky to clean up, I let Alana continue to hold her.

Becky and I quietly picked up and set the bed back to rights. I chucked my gloves in the biohazard can, then washed my hands at the sink.

"We'll give them a few minutes, then we can cut the cord and get the stats," I murmured to Becky as she came over.

I had the luxury of time in Cooper Valley. It was one of the enormous perks of the job. Sure, sometimes things got hectic at the hospital, but for the most part, we could take time with our patients, unlike where I'd done my residency in inner city Chicago.

"I told you this before, but I like the way you do things, Dr. Ames," she whispered.

"And I told you before, you need to quit that and call me Audrey," I replied, with a wry turn of my lips. It was a small town, and Becky had worked at the hospital for almost a decade. I wasn't going to insist the hospital staff call me Dr. Ames. I wasn't here for a power trip. Besides, she wasn't more than two years older than me, and I thought of her as a friend.

She smiled and waggled her eyebrows. "I forgot to tell you there's a giant bouquet of flowers at the nurses' station with your name on the card. From Jett Markle. Guess he's really smitten with you."

"Ugh." Why wouldn't he stop?

She snorted out a laugh. "Did you just say *ugh*?"

"Yes," I moaned, then remembered to keep my voice down. I moved to the doorway, and she followed. We didn't need to ruin a new family bonding moment detailing my unexciting dating life. "We had one date, and it wasn't great. I don't know why he won't get the hint."

"Not interested in the big shot rancher, huh? I thought you'd make a great couple."

I wrinkled my nose. "Why?"

She laughed and shrugged. "I don't know. You're the cute new doctor."

My scoff cut her off. As if. Doctor, yes. Cute, no.

"You heard me, the cute new *single* doctor in town, and he's the rich new rancher. I guess that's stupid." She gave me a thoughtful look. "If not him, then what's your type?"

The image of Boyd Wolf rose up in my mind, unbidden. Tousled sandy hair, sly smile, pale eyes, shoulders as wide as a doorway and abs ridged enough to climb. I couldn't forget those clever lips of his or that tongue...

Oh *gawd*. My nipples got hard beneath my scrubs just remembering all the things he'd done to me yesterday, and I crossed my arms over my chest. It was crazy. No, *I* was crazy. I had been then, letting him open my jeans, tug them down and get me off with a speed that had to be a record. In a barn. While there was lots of space on the property, I hadn't been all that quiet. I blushed, even now, with the possibility someone had overheard. I'd barely slept the night before thinking about it all. Reliving it. I'd even pulled out my vibrator to ease the ache, but the orgasm had been weak in comparison to what Boyd had wrung from me.

I was ruined for all other orgasms, that was for sure.

As for Boyd himself, he'd been into me. I remembered the way he touched me, kissed me, *licked* me. He'd been practically ravenous. *For me.* I doubted he was hard up for female companionship, and there were much more appealing women out there than me. I wasn't ever going to grow the extra seven or eight inches to be a supermodel. I could train for a marathon and still have a big butt. And unless I stopped down at the plastic surgeon's office, I wasn't ever going to offer more than small B boobs. But I'd seen how hard he'd been through his jeans. How pleased he'd been when I'd come. How he'd licked his fingers. *Licked his fingers!*

"Um, I like a cowboy, in theory, just not Jett. He was overbearing, condescending and a bore."

Becky huffed out a laugh. "Well, don't put too fine a point on it!"

"No kidding, right? You can have a volunteer take the flowers to one of the floors and give them to a patient without any visitors or family."

"You should come to Cody's tonight. You work way too many hours and haven't once joined us out for fun. How will you ever meet anyone if you only stay within these four walls? Wait, how did you meet Jett Markle, anyway?"

I rolled my eyes, gave Alana and family a glance, then looked to Becky. "Produce section at the grocery store. What's Cody's?" I asked.

She gave a light scoff. "See? The fact that you don't know the best—and only—local haunt for nightlife tells me you've been living like a hermit. Come out with me tonight. I'll introduce you to the *nice* cowboys. It'll be fun."

Once more, I tried to push the image of Boyd out of my mind. He wouldn't be one of the nice cowboys she wanted to introduce me to. Maybe someone like Abe. He was handsome and nice. And that was a good thing. Why then, was I so unexcited about the prospect of meeting anyone else? Why was I no longer interested in *nice?* That was so stupid. I definitely had to get out, get my mind *off* the sexy rodeo champ and meet the man of my dreams.

I glanced at the new family again. That was what I wanted. A doting husband, a new baby, the promise a brand-new family of three had for the future.

"You definitely should go," Alana said. I looked over in surprise to see her grinning at me. Her hair was slicked back with sweat, her cheeks flushed.

Her husband, who had his arm draped gently around his wife's shoulders, gave her a squeeze. "That's where we first hooked up."

I frowned in confusion.

"Yep. At Cody's. After my sister puked all over the dance floor." She laughed.

I went to grab a tiny knitted hat from a drawer. "All right," I said to Becky, surprising myself. "Let's do it, minus the throw up. What time?"

Becky smiled. "Let's say eight o'clock. Wear your cowgirl boots."

My smile drooped. "What if I don't have cowgirl boots?"

She elbowed me. "Kidding. I was kidding. You can wear anything you want, except scrubs."

I looked down at myself. "No problem."

"You should get a pair of cowgirl boots," Alana said, then kissed the top of her daughter's head. She had lots of dark hair like her father. "Don't you agree, Anabelle?"

"Anabelle," her husband choked. "It's perfect. She's perfect."

"She sure is." I went over and gave the hat to dad to slip on the newborn to help her stay warm. I grabbed new gloves from the dispenser on the wall, then clamped and cut the cord. Their happiness lifted me out of all my misgivings about proper attire or good-looking rodeo champs.

There was a new baby in the world, and her name was Anabelle. She was going to continue to bring endless joy to the world, simply by being alive.

If only everything was so miraculous and beautiful.

10

Boyd

"Here comes trouble," Levi, one of the ranch hands, muttered at the sound of hooves trotting up our drive. A bunch of us were sitting on the corral fence watching Sam, another of the ranch hands—and fellow pack member—tame the new stallion he'd bought.

It was always tricky at first. Horses that weren't foaled on the ranch had to get used to the shifter scent. Even the tamest of horses acted wild when we first brought them in. They didn't want to submit to humans that smelled like wolves.

I thought of Audrey, of how skittish she'd been the day before, how quickly she'd bolted after I'd tried to tame her. *With my tongue.* I shifted on the top rail, my dick getting hard without any room for it to fit.

I looked down the drive at the man riding toward us, squinting slightly into the bright sun. The day was hot, the sky blue. At least for now. Later in the afternoons, clouds usually built up over the mountains bringing storms.

Under the brim of his hat, I saw an unfamiliar face. I pegged him at late thirties. He rode stiffly, his spine straight, his hold on the reins too taut. He sure as fuck didn't know how to ride a horse.

"Who is that?" I murmured in case he was a shifter and had hearing as good as ours.

"Jett Markle," Rob replied, his voice as flat as usual. "He bought Didi's Double D ranch awhile back. The spread on the other side of Old Man Shefield's place."

I hadn't been back much in the decade since I'd graduated and bolted like a wild mustang, but I remembered Didi and why her place was called the Double D. I'd heard from Rob the place had sold but hadn't given it more thought. Until now.

"He's an asshole," Rob added, tipping his chin down but kept his gaze on the visitor. Markle was a human on pack land. Rob might appear calm, but I sensed the tightly coiled tension in him.

I took his comment with a grain of salt because shifters didn't think much of most humans. Rob, especially. He'd liked Old Man Shefield, our next door neighbor, but that was only because we'd known him since we were kids. We'd swam in his swimming hole. He'd been a good neighbor to our parents and offered a lot of support to Rob after they died. Even at eighteen, Rob hadn't accepted much help, but the guy had offered it nonetheless.

Markle trotted up and sat on his horse instead of dismounting. He didn't loosen his hold on the reins, despite the fact that they were no longer moving. "Howdy."

Rob sniffed, and I knew he was taking in the man on the wind. I picked up heavy cologne, soap and the tang of his sweat. Looking at him, I knew he wasn't from around these parts. While his clothes looked casual, they were expensive and too clean. No way he'd saddled the animal nor would he brush him down when he returned to his stable. Nah, he wouldn't want to muss his manicure. What fucker buffed his nails?

Levi and I waited for Rob, as our alpha, to respond first. Rob waited a beat, then another, like Markle wasn't worth his time. "How's it going?" Rob asked in the bored tone that implied he didn't give a shit how Markle answered.

"Not good. I think there's a wolf or wolves in these parts." He glanced behind us at the open land, as if he were looking now for the animals. "I saw prints on my land, and I'm missing one of my herd."

Rob bristled and the ripple of irritation ran through all of us. We were a pack, and pack animals were completely in tune with their alpha. Rob was blasting annoyance, and we'd all felt it.

Of course, Markle hadn't because he was just a human. Frail and inferior. And, clearly, an asshole.

I thought of a different human, much smaller and curvier. Sweeter and *not* an asshole. *Audrey,* my wolf whispered, missing her. I was going to do as Rob commanded and stick to her like fucking glue, but I knew she'd need some time. I'd got her off real good and needed to be patient for the chance to do it again.

I still didn't understand how it could be that my wolf had picked a human for us to mate, but the message was undeniable. Audrey Ames was mine.

"You found a carcass?" Rob demanded, stirring me from my thoughts. For once, I was thankful for his gruffness because it did a damned good job of killing the hard-on the thoughts of Audrey had brought about.

"No, but I'm missing one head."

"Probably wandered off."

Levi and I nodded our agreement.

No fucking way a wolf killed one of his cattle. There weren't any lesser wolves—what we called the plain wolves, the non-shifting variety—in the area because our pack had marked its territory. Sure, there were plain wolves in Montana, especially now since the rangers had released some in Yellowstone National Park, but not on Wolf Ranch. Not anywhere near Cooper Valley.

Shifter wolves were the dominants in the species. Lesser wolves would never hunt on our grounds. And a shifter would never kill a cow. We liked to eat beef, but on a roll with some cheese and ketchup like everyone else. Most of the pack were ranchers like us, and they knew better than to cause trouble with the locals that way. They might go out hunting, but they'd be killing deer or rabbits, not cattle.

The asshole was lying.

"It did not wander off," Markle snapped and his horse sidestepped in fear. He tugged on the reins which yanked at the bit in the animal's mouth. I had to stop the growl in my throat. None of us liked to see a horse mistreated, even through ignorance.

"I've never seen a wolf in these parts," Levi drawled, his outright lie bonding the rest of us to him. It was always us against them as far as pack policy with humans, and right now, we were very much against Markle. I couldn't see the city slicker out there on the range counting head every day. Unless he had three cows, I doubted he'd be able to tell one was gone.

"Yeah, me neither," Johnny said, the youngest of our pack, as he strode over from the stable. With him were two other guys, Clint and Joe. They must've heard the approach, heard some of the conversation, or at least their alpha's anger, from wherever they'd been working.

Markle glanced down at the twenty-year old and spluttered in anger. "I saw prints on my ride over here."

"On *your* property?" Levi asked in disbelief because none of us would've run on a human's land.

Rob shot Levi a look because his question was the wrong one to ask. Our story was that there were no wolves not that wolves hadn't been on Markle's property.

"Probably a dog's," I offered, to cover the mistake. "Our border collie might have ventured over your way. I think there's a bitch in heat down the road he's been howling to get at."

Markle shook his head. "It's a wolf. I came here to let you know because you have cattle, too. We need to organize a party and hunt the thing, or he's going to cull both our herds."

Levi let out a low growl beside me. I elbowed him in the ribs.

"I don't think that's necessary." I jumped off the fence and sauntered over to the asshole, turning on my charm. I tipped my hat back and looked up at him, absently patting his animal's sweaty neck. "But we'll keep an eye out. If we see any signs of wolf, we'll let you know."

Markle frowned at me. "Who are you?"

"That's Boyd, my younger brother," Rob said, stalking over to stand beside me. Even though I'd grown up and left the ranch, stood shoulder to shoulder in height, he still thought he needed to protect me.

"The rodeo champ," Markle commented, studying me in a different light. It was as if I had value, if only for being famous. "I've heard of you."

I wasn't surprised. It was a small town, and there wasn't

much to talk about. The fact that the nation's champion bull rider came from Cooper Valley was a source of pride for the human locals. The ones who didn't know there was no real reason to be impressed because I had nothing to fear from a pissed off bull. I actually had to hold myself back, or I'd give away that there was something very different about me. I'd been fine with it for a while, back when I was young and cocky. Well, cockier than I was now. It lost its appeal pretty fast when there was no goal besides having fun. Sure, the money was great, but my life had been... shallow. Just like the women I'd fucked.

I had a different goal now, and she wasn't shallow at all.

I tipped my hat. "Nice to meet you."

He scowled like the feeling wasn't mutual. Which was fine since I'd lied through my teeth, anyway. He turned his attention back to Rob. "We need to hunt this wolf. Now. I'm about to double the size of my ranch and—"

"What do you mean double?" Rob interrupted.

"I've got an offer in on the Shefield property. Old Shefield left it to a young niece who has no interest in ranching. From what the Realtor said, she's still in college and most likely won't be able to cover the cost of the taxes to keep the place. She'll take my offer. And then I'm going to double my herd."

I detected another growl from one of the guys behind us.

If I weren't standing so close, I'd be growling too. I hadn't taken much interest in Wolf Ranch since I'd been gone, but I sure as hell felt strongly about this. No fucking way we wanted Markle to be our next-door neighbor. Having one property between us was going to be bad enough, especially not with his stance on wolves.

We had to make sure that deal fell through.

"Well, if you guys won't track some wolves with me, I'll

rustle up some hunters at Cody's tonight," Markle said, scanning all of us. We weren't all here, but there were six of us, and we were all big. None of us liked him. He had to sense that, or he was as dumb as a nail in a fence post.

"Keep off this property, or we're going to have a problem," Rob growled. Yeah, Markle'd be pretty dumb to not miss his lack of welcome either.

Markle tensed, his lower jaw jutting out. "If I track the wolf over here, you're damn right I'm going to follow it to your property."

A low, collective growl rippled through the pack, every shifter suddenly stepping forward to flank their alpha and form a united front. This was the Wolf pack. No one fucked with us. We could take this one guy out, finish him and bury him in the back forty for no one to find for fifty years. Sadly, he'd probably be missed, maybe by his mother, and we didn't need anyone else snooping around.

"No. You won't." There was no mistaking the menace in Rob's voice.

Markle glared at Rob for a long moment, but there was nothing he could do. With an angry scoff, he yanked the reins to turn his horse around, then kicked its ribs and rode off without another word.

"Fucking dick," I muttered as soon as I deemed him out of earshot.

"You boys see what you can find out about those prints," Rob ordered.

"I'll bet they don't exist," Levi said. "You think it's true about Shefield's place? We can't have that asshole next door." He took his hat off, scratched the back of his neck, then settled it back in place.

Rob shook his head. "I sure as fuck hope not." He looked

at me. "You see if you can find anything out about it. Go to Cody's tonight, too. He seemed to like you the best."

I huffed at that. Totally doubtful, but I could use my fame to my advantage, at least with Markle.

"Make sure no one joins him on his hunt," he added.

I nodded, headed off toward the main house to shower. It was pathetic how buoyed I felt to have Rob give me a task for once. To trust me to handle something, other than the things I'd fucked up.

"I'm on it," I called.

Cody's it was. And maybe I'd find a little more out about my sweet doctor while I was mingling with the humans. My patience with giving her some space was pretty much over. My wolf, and dick, were in agreement on that one.

11

Audrey

I didn't know how to dress like a cowgirl. I had no boots. Definitely no hat. I'd settled on a button-down blouse—not flannel or even plaid, sadly—and a black jean skirt with a frayed hem that probably looked way more urban than western. It was the best I could do. I'd have to go shopping on my next day off for some real Montana clothes.

I left my hair long and ensured I had on makeup. I figured Becky would send me home or doctor me up with stuff from her purse in the bathroom mirror otherwise.

I was primped, spritzed and ready to have a good time.

The sun hadn't set yet—it stayed light late in the summer this far north—but the air was cooling off quickly. I parked my little car in between all the huge pickup trucks in the dirt lot outside Cody's and slung my purse over my shoulder to cross my body. I performed lifesaving surgeries and brought babies into the world. I was only walking into a bar for a little fun. There was nothing to be nervous about.

My palms were sweaty as I walked in the door, the blast of loud music and the scent of french fries and beer hit me hard. It was early still, so the place wasn't packed, but Becky was right that it was *the* place to be.

I took a quick glance around, looking for Becky. I'd purposely come a little late, so I wouldn't arrive first.

It had worked.

Becky stood at the bar holding a beer and talking with a tight cluster of people. She'd grown up in Cooper Valley and had many friends. I wasn't sure if it was a blessing or curse to run into someone you knew even if you were in the feminine hygiene aisle at the market. For me, I hoped to avoid Jett Markle in the produce section from now on.

I smiled and headed toward them and then nearly stopped short, my heart suddenly jammed up in my throat.

Was that Boyd Wolf at the bar?

At that moment, the cluster shifted, and I got a clear view of the rodeo champ, casually leaning against the sleek wood surface, a knot of women all around him. He spotted me at the same moment, and we locked gazes. It was like in the movies, where suddenly all the background sound became muffled. Like I had cotton in my ears.

A blast of conflicting emotions hit me at once. My knees went weak as if my body were already holding up and waving the white flag of surrender, calling out, *I'm yours, big guy! Come and get me!* At the same time, sharp irritation with the groupies pushing their big breasts out and leaning into his space brought on the bitter taste of jealousy—which wasn't like me at all. Add to that anger at Boyd for turning me into this mess of hormones, and I was one turned on and frustrated woman.

How dare he eat me out in his barn then flirt with a handful of other women! Sure, they were gorgeous, young and... gorgeous. Had he forgotten about me already? Yeah, he probably had.

The notch had been made, and he'd moved on. Fine. I could move on, too.

So I did what any self-respecting woman would do. No, not bolt for the door and go home to cry my eyes out over a carton of ice cream. I tossed my hair back and strutted over to Becky. I ignored Boyd completely.

As if that were possible because every guy I walked past wasn't as tall, as brawny or as imposing. None were as handsome or had the same lethal smile. None of them were Boyd.

He was at my elbow in a flash. "Hey there, darlin'. It must be my lucky night. I didn't know you would be here."

Color me blind, but I would've sworn he sounded sincere. Except that didn't make sense since I was able to see the women he'd left by the bar giving me death glares. They had their sights set on him. I didn't blame them, but I wanted to rip their eyes out. I'd thought we'd had a connection, but then that made me sound like a high schooler. The connection had been his mouth on my pussy. Nothing more. I was just another conquest for Boyd Wolf.

"I didn't know you would be here, either," I said primly, trying to angle my body more toward Becky.

Unfortunately, she wasn't picking up what I was putting down because she kept backing up and facing away, like she was giving me space to flirt with Boyd.

Dang it.

"What can I get you to drink?" he asked, his fingers circling my elbow and steering me toward the bar. The far side of the bar where the buckle bunnies weren't clustered.

"Oh, um..." I shook my head, trying to force some sense back into it. "I'll get my own drink. I don't want to keep you from your... friends."

Disappointment streaked across his expression but quickly disappeared as he leaned a little closer. "You're not going to punish me for not letting you give me that full examination, are you, Doc? I kind of liked examining you much better."

I turned to face the bar in the hope of hiding my blush. "Nope. I'm off-duty tonight, so you're off the hook. I won't bother you a bit, especially since you seem so... fit." I glanced down at his chest, which was clearly delineated in panty melting detail beneath a crisp white t-shirt. It was tucked into a pair of jeans that molded to every inch of his long legs and well-formed ass and nice bulge and... crap. Look higher at the belt buckle! It was huge, like a frisbee but in silver. Clearly, it was a championship something or other, but I didn't dare ask about it for sounding like an idiot.

I ordered a shot of Patrón and gave Boyd my back, stepping around to stand beside Becky and sticking out my hand to meet her friends. Friends who were ignoring me and staring wide eyed at Boyd. "Hi, I'm Audrey."

I shouldn't have been disappointed when Boyd took the hint and stepped away. I didn't actually see him do it, more like *felt* it. That had been my intention, to give him the cold shoulder, and yet I registered the loss of his nearness viscerally. My nipples hardened, and my pussy clenched as if telling me they wanted him back. They wanted his very skilled hands and mouth on them and didn't want to let the opportunity slip away.

My pussy had been in charge in Boyd's barn and while it got his head between my legs and a fantastic orgasm, that was all. Sure, I'd be using that for my vibrator-time fantasies for the rest of my life, but my bed wouldn't have Boyd in it because he'd be in some other woman's.

Tonight, I'd think with my mind, and my pussy would just have to deal. I tossed back the shot, then winced as the biting flavor went down hard and fast.

"Um, Audrey, you didn't tell me you knew Boyd Wolf," Becky said, her eyes shifting from me to somewhere over my shoulder where he'd gone. Probably back to his bunny hutch.

"He, uh, got hurt at the rodeo over the weekend. Remember I told you I was going to work the event?"

"Lucky girl," she replied, leaning in to be heard over the growing crowd and the music.

"Becky! He was hurt," I countered. I didn't like anyone to make light of a situation where someone had been injured.

"He doesn't look hurt to me," she said, licking her lips. As if she wanted not only a slice but the whole dang chocolate cake.

"His gaggle of girlfriends will take care of him." I tried to hide the hurt in my voice. I wasn't ready to tell her about my trip to Wolf Ranch or what happened in the barn.

She slowly shook her head as she sucked on the straw of her iced margarita. "I think he wants *you* to do that, and I don't mean heal any wounds he might have. I'm thinking he needs relief of a different kind."

My mouth dropped open as I stared at her. "I think you're very wrong."

She shook her head. "You might have the fancy medical degree, but I know men, and that one wants you. Don't deny you want him right back."

I stared at her. She stared at me. Her friends, thank God, were chatting between themselves, and I didn't have to explain this to them. "Fine. I do want him. But—"

She grinned and cut me off. "I'm so glad to hear that. Hi, Boyd."

I gasped, spun on my heel. Right there in front of my face was his chiseled chest. Oh. My. God.

Slowly, I tipped my chin up until I was looking into Boyd Wolf's gorgeous face, split by his signature grin. "The feeling's mutual, darlin'. Sorry for stepping away, I needed to get my beer." He held up a longneck between his fingers.

"I... I thought—" I thought a sinkhole should open up and swallow me, but that wasn't going to happen.

"I thought we had a good time yesterday." He winked.

"Yesterday?" Becky asked. "Wasn't the rodeo over the weekend?"

"It was, but I couldn't resist myself." Boyd tipped his head in my direction. "This woman's got me on my knees with want."

While Boyd spoke to Becky, his words were meant just for me.

I blushed and shook my head. I'd gone to Wolf Ranch to check on him but hadn't done so. Instead of me getting him out of his shirt to see where the bull had struck him, *he'd* gotten me out of my pants... and panties.

He wasn't injured. I'd clearly been wrong. Unless he had an ingrown toenail, I couldn't see a thing wrong with the guy. He definitely didn't look like someone who'd been gored by a bull.

I didn't understand it, but the proof of it was him standing before me.

"I'm sorry, Boyd, but this isn't my thing."

"What isn't?"

I hardened my resolve. "You're a fun time. But I'm looking for something serious. And you're not sticking around." I pointed at him and circled my finger, directly at his huge belt buckle, which blatantly indicated his profession and imminent return to the circuit.

There. I made it about his job, not that I thought he was a man-whore. Although why I believed he had feelings that required sparing was beyond me. A guy like him probably had this conversation fifty times a year. I'd looked up the rodeo circuit schedule, and it covered half the west over a six month span.

Boyd looked chagrined by my words, but I didn't want to read too much into that. He wasn't getting lucky tonight with me. He'd survive. Since he could probably talk the underpants off a nun if given the chance, I decided fleeing was my best strategy.

"Excuse me," I said, then beelined for the bathroom, hiding in there for as long as I could.

When I came out, I was relieved to see Becky nearby with no sign of Boyd. Well, relieved, but also disappointed. Not in myself or Boyd because it wasn't his fault he was a player but that the chemistry was impossible to resist. I *wanted* to hang out with him, maybe even have a little fling, but I knew it was better to cut him out now than to be hurt later. I took a breath, headed toward Becky.

I didn't make it to her side.

Jett Markle, Mr. Bad Date, stepped in my path, a smug grin on his face.

12

Audrey

"Audrey, so great to see you." Jett reached out and clasped my shoulder. He probably thought he was showing warmth, but it was everything I could do not to flinch. He and Boyd were of similar size, but while I felt protected by Boyd, Jett felt imposing. The fact that he hadn't gotten the idea that the first date was also the *only* date creeped me out. Fortunately, we weren't alone. The bar was now packed.

"I'll buy you a drink." His grip propelled me to the bar. Damn, could the guy be any pushier?

Seriously.

I assumed this was how he made it big in the hedge fund world.

Considering I just turned down a far more appealing drink offer, I found it hard to even be polite. I dug in my heels and resisted his hold on me, which made my arm tug in its socket. "No, Jett. I don't want a drink with you." My action and loud words attracted the attention of everyone around us. I usually didn't want to be the center of attention, but now I was glad for it.

He stopped and turned to look down at me, but he didn't let go of my shoulder.

"I'm here with a friend," I said.

Before I finished speaking, I felt a hand on my lower back and knew instantly who it was.

"Everything okay here, darlin'?" Boyd's voice was soft and slow, but there was no mistaking the danger in it. The menace to Jett if I said things weren't okay.

I was one hundred and five percent sure Boyd would happily deck the guy if I wanted. What I wasn't sure of was whether he'd hold back, even if I told him things were fine. I didn't want to start a fight. I didn't want Jett to think he was being interrupted. I'd told him we were one and done and that hadn't worked. If I told Boyd I was fine and went about my night with Becky, I had a feeling Jett would keep sending flowers, keep texting. Or worse.

There was one, very big, very tall way to get my point across to Jett that I wasn't interested.

I turned and placed my hand on Boyd's hard chest. His arm instantly banded around my waist, drawing me closer. "There you are!" I purred, like we were together. As in *together*. I stared adoringly up into his face.

Boyd looked down at me, and his easy smile came immediately, but his gaze was shrewd. I'd just told him things weren't going to work out, and now I was fawning all over him. He might be crazy enough to climb on the back of a bull and try to stay on, but he was no idiot. His gaze traveled between me and Jett. "Was this guy bothering you, darlin'?"

"No, just a misunderstanding. I was just telling him that

it wasn't necessary to text me or send me flowers at work. Our dinner last weekend was a one-time thing."

"Is that so?" Boyd asked.

I nodded. "Yes, clearly Jett didn't know you were my date." I laid my cheek against his muscled chest like we were far more than dating—like we were an exclusive couple.

Too bad that wouldn't be the case.

Jett's eyes narrowed, and his cheeks flushed with anger. He stared at me, but the hatred was focused over my head at Boyd. Obviously, he wasn't used to losing the girl to a rival.

"Aw, that right?" Boyd cradled the side of my head, his thumb lightly brushing over my ear. It was way too intimate a gesture—and I liked it way too much—but he was playing along with me, acting the part of my boyfriend. "I didn't realize another man was sending my girl text messages. Especially ones she doesn't want."

Wow, he was protective. I liked the feeling of not being the responsible one, the one who had to take care of herself, and hell, everyone around her. It was my job to help people in life and death scenarios, and in this one thing, it felt amazing to hand it off to Boyd. Crazy, but amazing. I wanted to laugh at Jett, but that would only make things worse.

What if Boyd could be boyfriend material? some silly voice in my head whispered.

But no. I mentally shook off that ridiculous idea. I already knew he couldn't. He was surrounded by women at the rodeo, and he'd been surrounded when I got to the bar. A guy like that didn't fall for a dorky small-town doctor like me.

But Boyd was the kind of guy if you gave him an inch, he took a mile, because the next thing I knew, he'd tilted my face up to his and brushed his lips across mine.

My eyes fell closed, and I gave in to the slightest contact. *Oh my.*

"Happy to be your huckleberry, darlin'," he murmured.

I flushed and looked to see if Jett was watching, but instead I saw his back as he stalked off toward the pool tables.

I pushed at Boyd's rock-solid chest. "Thanks, but I think I'm safe now." *Safe from Jett, but not from you.*

"He didn't hurt you, did he? Now or on your date?"

I shook my head. "We went to dinner last weekend. I met him at the restaurant. Nothing happened. I told him I wasn't interested in more, but he didn't get the message."

"Texts? Flowers?"

"Yes. But thanks to you, I think he has the idea now."

Boyd looked over my shoulder in Jett's direction. "You have any more trouble with him, I want to know." His gaze dropped to mine. "You hear?"

Nodding, I replied, "Yes, thanks. For all your help with Jett."

I turned, scanning the bar for Becky. Music came from a jukebox or speakers somewhere, but a band was setting up on the stage.

Boyd had only loosened his arm around me, but it was still there, keeping my body in close proximity to his. *Very* close proximity, as in a piece of paper wouldn't fit between us. "Running again? You know, I'm a champion steer roper. I'm skilled with a lasso and catching things." He'd leaned down, so his mouth was right by my ear. I shivered, not only from his lips brushing over the swirl of my upper ear but from the idea of Boyd tying me up.

I spun about, ready to tell him off, shoving my finger in his chest. Instead, since he'd been bent down to speak, when I turned, his face was right there. Our noses bumped, our mouths almost brushed. He smelled of a hint of soap, no aftershave for him, and the tang of beer.

Maybe it was the shot of tequila or his closeness, but it was suddenly hot in the bar. "I... I didn't know that," I replied, unsure of what to say. I couldn't back up, or I'd bump people behind me. If I moved forward, I'd be kissing Boyd.

No kissing Boyd! I had no idea where those lips had been since yesterday and between my thighs. Oh shit, now I was thinking of those lips on me. *There.*

A shrill whoop cut through the crowd, and we turned to look where it had come from. Over the heads of the crowd, Becky was riding on what appeared to be a bull. Her arm was flung over her head, and her long hair flew out behind her. No wonder I hadn't seen her, I'd been looking the wrong way.

"There's a mechanical bull?" I asked, staring at my friend. Somehow, I'd missed the bull before now, perhaps because it was in the back of the bar, and no one had been on it. With Becky sitting on top of it, she could be easily seen over everyone's heads. I'd had no idea my friend could ride a bull. At least a fake one.

"Sure is. You want to try?" Boyd had stood to his full height and settled a hand on my shoulder.

"Faster!" Becky shouted and the bull's pace picked up. She whipped about, then after about two seconds, fell off. I couldn't see her through the crowd, but I assumed there were big pads for her to land upon.

"Come on, let's check it out."

Boyd steered me through the throng to the low rail that separated the mechanical bull from the main bar area.

Becky was pushing herself to her feet on the thick padding that circled the mechanical bull, smiling and laughing. She gave me a wave then headed toward the bar. She had to be fairly buzzed to climb on that thing in the first place. I knew I wouldn't see her again tonight, playing wingman by staying away from me and Boyd.

Whatever. I focused on the now empty machine.

"No horns," I observed, and Boyd laughed.

"No horns," he repeated, rubbing a hand over the spot where he'd been bleeding just the other day. "But it's still one hell of a ride." He gave an ear-splitting whistle. "Russell, she's up next."

I glanced up at Boyd, who was looking across the cordoned off area to, I assumed, Russell, who was running the controls for the bull. I lifted my gaze and saw he was pointing down at my head.

"What? No way. I can't go on that thing." Nervously, I tucked my hair behind my ears.

"Sure, you can."

I shook my head. "No, Boyd. I can't."

He frowned. "Why not?"

His light eyes held mine. He wasn't joking with me, he seriously didn't understand.

"I'll go, Boyd." A pretty young thing came up to the rail and gave Boyd a *I'll ride the mechanical bull now and show you my moves so I can ride you later* look. She was tall, thin, big boobed and left nothing to hide beneath her clothing choice. Painted on jeans. A plaid button up that was missing half the buttons and tied in a neat little bow over her bare belly. A belly that should have a label like cottage cheese that said Fat Free!

"You know I'm good for a wild ride," she added, as she kicked one leg over the fence. She straddled it, paused and winked—*gag!*—then flung her other over and made her way up and onto the bull. I could have sworn Boyd growled, but it was hidden a little by my hatred by little Miss Perfect and Slutty. She winked, not at Boyd, but at me.

Yeah, I hated her.

She signaled and the bull started up. She moved with the machine's forward and backward motion. She'd done this before, but I knew that. She was not a virgin at anything.

People lined the rail to clap and cheer but also to probably watch and see if her breasts popped from the limited confines of her shirt. The ride lasted longer than eight seconds and so did the button dexterity on her top. She climbed down and sauntered our way. Yes, sauntered.

"That's how it's done."

Yeah. Total bitch.

"Want to go for our own ride now, Boyd?" she purred.

Boyd looked to me and shook his head. "Nope. I've got what I want right here."

I couldn't see her around Boyd's body, but I heard her huff.

"Don't you want to go off with her?" I asked.

He frowned down at me, didn't even look Total Bitch's way when she stomped off.

"Why would I want to do that?" he asked.

"Um, because she's gorgeous and is way more skilled than I am." I wasn't just talking about riding a bull.

"Oh, when you get going, you're pretty wild yourself," he countered, reaching up and stroking my cheek.

I narrowed my eyes at the simple gesture. "Yeah, well. Me, yesterday. Her, today. It's fine."

I started to turn away, but he spun me back with a gentle grip on my upper arm. "No, it's not fine. I think I've been pretty clear that I want you. Only you. What makes you think I'm into bed hopping?"

I pushed my glasses up my face and stared at him. "Um, because you do. Bed hop, I mean."

He rubbed the back of his neck and glanced away. "Okay, in the past. But that was then. This is now."

"You're reformed? What, did you hit your head when you fell off that bull?" I wondered.

"When a guy meets the right girl." He looked over his shoulder and signaled to Russell. "Your turn. I want to see what you've got."

"Boyd, I can't."

"Audrey, you can."

"Boyd, I'm wearing a skirt."

He looked down. Stared at my skirt. My legs. And stared some more. "Yes, you are."

"Boyd—" I began, then saw Total Bitch leaning against the rail, smirking. She wasn't right behind Boyd but close enough that I knew she was waiting for her chance to pounce.

Fine. I couldn't turn into a supermodel, but I could get on the back of a mechanical bull and show her I had some moves of my own. False pride, for sure. But a woman had to do what a woman had to do.

Maybe Boyd saw the shift in me, the determination, because he set his hands on my hips and lifted me up and over the rail as if I weighed nothing. I stared down the bull as if it were real and not mechanical.

"Climb up there," Boyd instructed.

I made my way onto the padding, careful not to flash anyone. Fortunately, my skirt hit just a few inches above my knee, not the tiny Band-Aid sized ones some ladies were wearing. When I stood beside the bull, I looked over my shoulder. I had no idea how to get on it. There was no way to toss my leg over, not unless I wanted to chuck my modesty right along with it.

Boyd swung himself over the rail and climbed up beside me. He leaned down and cupped his hands together to make a step. "Put your left foot here, then swing your right over."

People were shouting and hollering for me to hop on, but Boyd didn't pay them any attention. I looked at him for a second, then at his clasped hands. He wasn't making fun of me. He was helping. I wasn't sure if he wanted me to do this for him or for myself. I knew I was doing this for myself, not Boyd. I wasn't going to feel less than Total Bitch. I might fall off the stupid fake animal, but at least I tried. And as long as my skirt didn't ride up to my waist when I did it, I'd be able to remain in town instead of moving to a different state.

I set my foot in his hold and followed his instructions and was sitting astride the mechanical bull before I could say thanks. Even though my skirt only drifted up to mid-thigh, I tugged at the hem, then looked around and had a full view of the entire bar. It was higher up than it seemed from the other side of the railing.

"Good girl," Boyd said, smiling at me. This smile wasn't sly. It wasn't sexy. It was... warm, as if it was a new kind—just for me. "You got this?"

Even though he'd practically goaded me up here, he wasn't going to make me go through with it. I nodded though. Now that I was sitting on the bull, I wanted to do it. I even heard Becky holler, "Way to go, Audrey! Ride that bull."

"Nice and slow," I instructed Boyd. I wasn't going to pretend I could ride like Total Bitch.

"Yeah, nice and slow is just right."

He wasn't talking about bull riding.

His big hand slid down my thigh, from the top half covered in the jean skirt to lower down where the material had ridden up. I felt the callouses, the warmth. In that moment, Boyd wasn't a cocky rodeo champ. He was Boyd, the man who had eyes only for me.

I took a deep breath and took off my glasses and handed them to him. Besides not wanting them to break, it was probably better not being able to see anything, or anyone.

He stepped back. Only when he was back over the rail did the bull kick in, just like my racing heart. I just had to hope it wouldn't break when I fell, and I didn't mean off the bull.

13

Boyd

I GAVE Russell a look that threatened *don't hurt my woman*. He saw it, clenched his jaw and nodded. The bull started up, so slow that it was like Audrey was on the kiddie horse that cost a penny to ride at the grocery store. When someone to my left shouted to speed it up, I whipped my head his way and glared, throwing off all the wolf energy I had, even though he was human. The guy turned and walked away from the rail. *The fucker.*

The bar was packed. People walked by and slapped me on the shoulder in greeting. I paid them no attention. I could only see Audrey. Hell, if a fight broke out behind me, I doubt I'd know. I certainly wouldn't care.

Audrey's bare knees tightened on the bull's sides, and her knuckles went white around the handhold. The bull's pace increased, but it was a slow adjustment, and she seemed to be doing okay. When it moved a little faster, her motions became awkward.

"Go with it. Relax. Lift your free arm up in the air to counteract the motion," I instructed, and she did as I said, her movement improving. Ten seconds. Twenty. Thirty. She wasn't going to stay on going much faster though. I could see it in every line of her body—and I was watching every single curvy line—and the way she was tiring.

It didn't look like strenuous work hanging on for only eight seconds, but Audrey had been on for much longer, and the mechanical bull's faux leather was pretty fucking slippery. I doubted I'd be able to stay on if I had to wear a dang skirt and ride the thing.

I sliced my hand back and forth across my throat, indicating to Russell to shut 'er down. The bull immediately slowed, then came to a stop. I didn't hop the rail like I wanted but let her carefully kick a leg over then slide down and off on her own. She stumbled when the soft mat gave beneath her feet and put a hand on the side of the bull to steady herself.

When she came over to the rail, I flipped opened the sides of her glasses and carefully set them over her ears. "You did it, darlin'. In a skirt, no less."

Relief must've made her a little punch drunk because she let out a breathy laugh. "I did, didn't I? Not quite as good as—"

"Better," I interrupted. I knew she was comparing herself with Karen, the show-off who went before her, but the truth was, there was no comparing. Karen was a backwoods shifter from one of the families living up in the mountains. She'd moved to town when she was eighteen, probably in hopes of snagging one of the Wolf brothers as a mate, but obviously that never took. Rob wasn't interested in any woman. He wasn't gay, but he hadn't met his mate yet. He'd have to soon. I was starting to feel the itch of moon madness, and I was the youngest of the three of us. I'd think he was slowly losing his shit right about now. Not that he'd let on. As for Colton, he was in the military out in North Carolina. I hadn't seen him in years although not because I avoided him. His leave and my breaks from the rodeo rarely coincided. Karen wasn't going to ever have luck with him unless she hopped a plane east.

As for me? Not happening. Never had, never would. I knew who I wanted. Who my wolf wanted, and she was standing right in front of me.

I needed to show Audrey exactly how superior she was to every female here. I also needed to somehow prove to her she wasn't another notch on my bedpost as she thought. She definitely had me filed in the player category.

The trouble was, there wasn't much evidence against that theory at this point. When she'd walked in, I'd been flanked by four women, all eager to get in my pants. A previous night, I'd have taken any one of them up on her offer. If she asked around, everyone in town who knew me would attest that I was a one-and-done kind of guy.

Dammit. It wasn't because I wasn't into the long haul with one woman, I just had never come across her before. I was no monk, so the women I'd slept with in the past had been fun. And that was it.

But now... fuck. I'd screwed up. Big time. I needed to get off the distract-her-with-sex train and get to know her. All of her, not just that beautiful, curvy body. To be her best friend. Not because Rob ordered me to but because that's what mates were. Everything to each other.

Why did that suddenly make me feel like she was out of my league?

Because she was smart—a doctor—and here I hadn't even been to college. I practically burned rubber getting off the ranch at eighteen to join the rodeo circuit, and I never looked back. Up until now, I'd relied heavily on my physical prowess and my ability to charm the panties off every female in a three-mile radius. I'd had no skin in the game in the past. I'd been having fun, spreading orgasms across the country. I hadn't been trying to make anyone fall in love with me. I hadn't found my mate.

Now I was face-to-beautiful-face with her.

"Are you going to ride it?" she asked, her eyes glassy as she stared up at me through her sexy-as-fuck glasses. She was slightly tipsy, which I loved, but it made my job of proving I was into more than just pounding between those sweet thighs of hers even harder.

"Me? No." I grinned.

"Oh, right. Of course not. You're still hurt, right?" Her palm brushed over my side, like she was seeking the wound, so I flinched away. I couldn't have her discovering there was no injury. In fact, I should probably put a bandage on the area next time I was with her. Especially since I was hoping we'd be naked and horizontal for that reunion.

"You want another drink?" I asked.

She shook her head. "No. I'm driving. Have to sober up."

"I'll get you a bottle of water, then. Stay here." I started to leave her, then turned back. "On second thought, I don't trust Markle not to bother you." I took her hand. "Come with me, darlin'."

Her laugh was low and throaty. A normal human probably wouldn't have been able to hear it over the music, but I did. It sounded like warm summer rain. A full moon run. Sunset on the back of a horse.

I elbowed my way in at the bar and charmed a female

out of her stool before she realized it was for another woman. Then I picked my sweet doctor up by the waist, lifted her, and plopped her down on the stool. I shifted slightly so my thigh was between her knees.

Yeah, I might've been showing off my strength more than I should. But she was tipsy from the one shot of tequila, and I guessed not tremendously experienced with men. I didn't think she'd notice or remember how easily I could manage her weight.

I ordered two bottles of water and slid my body closer to hers, the heat from her inner thighs on mine, my hand at her lower back. "How'd you end up in Cooper Valley, Doc?"

The bartender returned with the drinks, and I cracked open a lid on one and handed it to her. She drank a few sips, then rubbed her full lips together. "I always wanted to live somewhere this beautiful. I love the mountains. And the sky. It's so big here in Montana."

I smiled. Big Sky Country was certainly Montana's motto, but she'd said it with reverence that I suddenly saw the area through her eyes. It was true, the expanse of open blue sky against the rugged mountains made this a magnificent place to live. Sometimes I forgot how lucky I had it having a place, a home... a fucking pack, to return to.

"Where are you from?"

"I grew up in Columbus, Ohio. But I moved from Chicago, where I did my residency."

"What's your area of expertise?"

"I'm an ObGyn."

Oh yes. I should have remembered that from a comment she made when we met. "You deliver babies?"

"Among other responsibilities."

"You picked the right field."

"How so?"

I leaned on my elbow to consider my words. It seemed important I get this right, and I was out of my element. "I imagine you bring a lot of joy into this world."

Her smile burst open like a blooming flower, and my chest warmed. She leaned forward, and the intense pleasure I experienced at having her full attention made it easy not to succumb to the temptation of looking down at her sweet cleavage. "That's exactly why I love my job. Every baby is a tiny miracle. I feel so honored to help usher them into the world."

I reached for her hand and squeezed it. "It was probably best that the rodeo guys you helped didn't know you treat pregnant women and deliver babies. Might hurt their big egos."

Apparently, that was the wrong thing to say because her smile dimmed, and she pulled her hand back. I tried to figure out what I'd said wrong, but it then became apparent.

"Remember, you can't go back to the rodeo until you've had a full physical." She drew a breath like she was going to continue on her lecture, but I interrupted.

"I may not go back." I scratched the back of my neck, eyed the guy who was riding the mechanical bull, then looked back at her. "I'm, ah, hoping I find a reason to stay."

Her eyes widened, and those full lips parted. Then her gaze dropped to her bottle of water, and she took a hasty drink, the droplets dribbling down her chin. "That's laying it on a little thick, don't you think?" she muttered.

Reaching out, I wiped the water away with my thumb. "Let me show you around, Audrey. Tomorrow."

"Is that code for something?"

I shook my head. "No, Doc. I want to spend time with you." I leaned in, so only she could hear my next words. "With our pants on. Maybe I got a little hasty at the barn, but I won't apologize. I really want to know you better. Is that so strange?"

She met my gaze and finished off her water. "Um, I guess not." Her gaze dropped again. "I work early tomorrow for a few scheduled patients, but I'm free after two, unless someone goes into labor."

I couldn't stop the giant smile from stretching across my face. Relief was swift, and my wolf practically high fived me. "Great. I'll see you then. Maybe you should get home and get some rest if you're working early."

She peered up at me like she was trying again to decide if I was speaking in code but then slid off the bar stool. I stepped back to give her room. "Yes, I think I'm ready to drive."

"I'll follow you home, just to be sure you make it safely."

Understanding dawned on her face, followed by a little smirk and flick of her brows. She didn't believe me. Dammit. I wanted to have sex with her. Now. Later. Anytime. *All* the time. But it wasn't going to happen tonight. It couldn't.

Trouble was, my dick had already leaped into painful action. No, that wasn't the real trouble. The real trouble was that I wasn't going to get him into the action. For once, I was thinking with my big head not my little one. My dick could get hard for Karen—what conscious male's wouldn't—but my mind only wanted Audrey, and that was a first.

My dick would stay in my pants, at least until tomorrow.

Tomorrow, once we'd had some time to get to know each other, all bets were off. I'd get to know all kinds of things about her, like if the back of her knees were an erogenous zone. If her nipples were really sensitive. If she liked to be on top or if she liked the nice deep thrust taking it from behind could give her.

I escorted her outside and into her car, then climbed in

my truck and followed her home. I wasn't going to get out of the truck. It was a bad idea. But the gentleman in me couldn't stand not jumping out to open her door and help her out of the car.

Unfortunately, the moon was waxing, and my wolf made it hard to contain my lust for her. Her sweet scent being kicked up on the evening breeze didn't help for shit.

"Wow," she breathed staring up at me. "Your eyes almost glow in the moonlight."

Fuck.

I blinked rapidly and looked away. "Do they?" I made a sound somewhere between a cough and a laugh. "Weird."

Tell her, my wolf whispered.

That was a crazy fucking idea because telling her was forbidden. Rob wanted me to stick close to her, so we'd know if she suspected the truth, not to tell it to her outright.

Then again, mating her would be a giveaway, too, and I was already on board with that.

Mark her, my wolf growled.

I took a step back. I couldn't mark her. Why had I not considered that until this moment? Oh fuck. She wouldn't survive a mating bite. I could sever an artery, and she could bleed out. Even if I didn't, it would be painful for her and would leave a terrible scar on her delicate human flesh.

I looked down at her. So small. Fragile. Perfect. She wasn't a twig like most women who crossed my path. No, she had some meat on her bones. To my wolf, she was healthy to rear pups. To me, she had something to grab onto, to sink into when I fucked her until she screamed my name. She was all female. Her breasts were small beneath her cute top, but real. I wondered if her nipples were tiny or large, pink or coral. Upturned or flat saucers to be licked.

My wolf and I knew her pussy. Her scent, her taste, the hot, wet clench. So fucking tight. Musky.

She was staring up at me with those fathomless blue eyes, such a contrast to her dark hair. The lenses of her glasses only amplified their size, how open and trusting she was. Innocent. Perfect.

Marking her was out of the question. I could never do such a violent thing to her. I scrubbed my hand over my face. No mark, no mate. No mating, and it would just be fucking. Just what she didn't want. I couldn't fuck her and *not* mate her.

Wait. Something was wrong here. Why would my wolf want to mate a human? Why was he so fucking insistent that she was the one? No other wolf I knew was mated to a human.

It just wasn't done.

This didn't make sense.

But Audrey hadn't noticed any of my mental mind fuck. She stepped into my space. "I know I said I didn't want a fling, but... God. I owe it to women everywhere. Are you coming in?"

Yes, growled my wolf.

My dick surged against the zipper of my jeans.

But for once in my life, I wasn't going to screw this up. I moved slowly, so I could keep control. I didn't want my wolf to take over, and fates knew I felt him scratching right at the surface, ready to show his fangs and embed my scent into her skin forever. I cupped the back of her head and leaned down, brushing my lips across hers lightly.

"I want to," I murmured. "Fuck, I really want to. But you need your rest. And this is me showing you I'm interested in more than sex."

The disappointment on her face nearly killed me. Or

maybe that was the throbbing in my balls. Either way, I was dying.

Even with only the glow of the street light, I could see her embarrassment. She'd told me no earlier, that she wasn't like the Karens out there. Now, she'd offered herself up, and I turned her down. I was an asshole no matter what I did here.

"Give me your phone," I said, my voice gravelly with need. And frustration.

She handed it to me, and I called myself with it and handed it back. "Now you have my number. Let me know if you have a sweet baby to deliver, otherwise I'll be here to pick you up at three. Got it?"

I didn't give her a chance to answer because kissing her hard suddenly became way more important. I wrapped my lips around hers, claiming that mouth like my life depended on it. Like this was the way I marked a human. My tongue swept between her lips, tangled with her. Gripping the back of her head, I angled her as I wanted, drinking from her.

When I broke the kiss, her glasses were crooked, and she wore a dazed expression. Her fingertips travelled to her lips, as if feeling to see if they were still there. Or how swollen they were.

Yeah, I knew just how she felt.

I took her keys from her and opened the front door of her small but sweet cottage. She lived a few blocks off Main Street in the older section of town. Trees and plantings were well established, and I scented honeysuckle along with her peach essence. I guided her through the doorway.

"Now get some sleep," I said, slapping her ass.

"Oh!" she exclaimed, looking over her shoulder with a startled but pleased expression.

I grinned and made a note: *likes spanking.*

Well, that was good because I *fucking loved* her ass.

"Goodnight, darlin'."

"Goodnight, cowboy." Her breathy voice made it so fucking hard to back away and leave.

But I did.

Because Audrey Ames mattered to me. And I was going to prove it to her.

14

Audrey

There was no way I was going to be able to sleep. I rolled over, tugged at the blanket that got wrapped around me. Groaned in frustration. I'd showered and got ready for bed. Analyzed every second of the night. Jett Markle. Using Boyd as my fake date. God, I'd ridden a mechanical bull! Boyd's goodbye kiss. All of it.

I stared at the way the moonlight made shapes on the ceiling.

No. Sleep wasn't coming. Not after what Boyd had just done to me. One kiss and my entire body was in flames. One slap on my ass, and I was ready to hump my pillows all night long.

He'd spanked me! I'd been stunned by that but more stunned because I'd liked it. Holy crap, had I liked it. But he'd left me wanting. Reaching back, I cupped my bottom where his hand had struck. Earlier, I'd peeked in the mirror, and there was a pink Boyd-sized handprint on my ass. It was as if he'd stuck with me even after he'd left.

I'd almost died on the spot when he'd turned me down. All night long, I'd told him no. I'd outright said he was a player, then I'd decided to hell with it. He was God's gift to women, and I owed it to all of them to get it on with him. After the whole incredible encounter in his barn, I knew he was a giver. He hadn't wanted me to get him off. He'd gotten on his knees for me, not the other way around. Most man whores—although I didn't really know very many—wanted a woman to get him off, give him a blow job and be done.

He had to have blue balls by now. I'd felt how hard he was when he'd pressed up against me in the bar. He'd wanted me all along. The kiss hadn't been a lie. But if he really was a one-night stand kind of guy, why had he walked away? Why had he said no? What player said no?

Maybe Boyd wasn't a player. No, he'd admitted he was. Or had been. Maybe he really was trying to be different with me.

Still, while I appreciated his reasons, it was still cruel of him not to come in and satisfy me after he got me all worked up. I must be ovulating. Becky would say I was horny.

Well, she was right. My nipples were hard, my pussy ached with want.

How dare he leave me all hot and bothered! He wasn't a man whore. He was a tease. I intended to tell him so when I saw him tomorrow.

Screw that. I was telling him now. I grabbed my phone from the nightstand and opened a text message for his number.

Well, that was my intention, but I guess I hit dial, instead, because suddenly the phone was ringing.

Oops! Um... I hung up quickly, then laughed out loud at

myself. That was stupid. God, I felt like a high school girl. Should I call him back?

No need. He called me.

"Oh, um, hi Boyd!" The laughter came through in my voice as I set the phone by my ear. I lay in my bed, the room dark and quiet, and I talked to a boy. No, a man. Boyd Wolf was *all* man.

"Hey darlin'. I was just thinking about you. Actually, never stopped. Everything okay? Jett Markle's not messing with you some more, is he?" His deep velvety rumble reached straight into my body, heating me from the core. And his concern... gah.

"No. I'm fine. I was just going to tell you that it was mean of you to get me all worked up and then just leave. I'm too revved up to sleep now!"

"Yeah, I was just trying to let off a little steam myself."

My nipples hardened to diamond points. I pictured him lying on his bed, his cock in hand. "Y-you were?"

"Uh huh. I'm sorry to leave you aching, darlin'. But I had to bust up your ideas about me."

"M-my ideas?" I still couldn't get past the image of him stroking himself. I wanted to see that cock up close and in person. I wanted to help with my mouth and tongue. What was wrong with me? I'd wanted sex before but never had lusty thoughts about a BJ.

"That I only want in those lacy little panties. Which I do —no denying it. But I meant it when I said I was interested in sticking around here if there was a good reason. And I'm hoping that reason will be you."

I didn't know what to say for a second.

"That's insane." I sounded breathless. "You just met me. You don't know anything about me. You couldn't possibly want to stay and settle down with me."

No, he hadn't said *settle down*. But wasn't that what he meant?

"You don't believe in love at first sight, Doc?" he asked, his voice deep and rich like dark coffee through the phone.

My breath left me in a whoosh. What was he saying? "I-is that what you feel for me? Love?"

"From the moment I saw you in that med room at the arena. I almost lost my shit when Abe invited you out for coffee. After, in the stands, he put his hand on your shoulder, I saw red."

"You were on the bull!" I remembered it clearly.

"I'm possessive, Audrey Ames. Like I said, from the first moment I saw you. Even Abe, who's a good guy, shouldn't have touched you."

"You're crazy!" I tried to laugh it off, but butterflies were taking wing in my belly.

"Then I found out you live in my hometown? It can't be coincidence, darlin'. It was meant to be."

Meant to be.

Goosebumps ran up and down my arms. "*This* is crazy." The words tumbled out on a laugh.

"Mmm." His deep rumble was pure sex. I thought I detected the slap of flesh and almost moaned at the thought of him abusing himself over me right now. "You know what's not crazy?"

"What?"

"Phone sex." Apparently, he read minds. "Me getting you off right now. Are you in bed?" he asked.

"Uh huh." I tried to make my voice sound sexy although that was never really my game. I was not the sex kitten type. I was a doctor. We used clinical names for body parts and didn't sexualize any of it.

"I've never had phone sex before," I admitted.

"Well, that's a shame. You've been missing out. Don't worry, I'll pop that cherry for you right now."

He wanted phone sex. Now. With me. Oh. My. God.

I could get on board with this. He'd kept his end of the deal and hadn't slept with me. He was being a gentleman. Well, maybe not that exactly because... yeah, phone sex.

But I wasn't a prude. I liked sex. I'd loved what Boyd had done to me in his barn and knew he'd be good at other things, too. This was like a man whore compromise. He'd prove he could hold off and yet wanted to have a little fun anyway.

I switched the phone to speaker and set it on the bed near my pillow, then slid one hand under my camisole and squeezed my own breast. My nipple was rock hard. Maybe this was a good way to go with him. I wasn't anything like those buckle bunnies. I had body issues, and if he got me naked, I'd be distracted by what he saw... the dimples on my thighs, my non-centerfold boobs.

"I want you to take your clothes off, darlin'. Will you do that for me?"

I didn't know why that sounded so naughty. I guessed because I didn't normally sleep in the nude. I wriggled out of my pajama shorts and pulled the top off, then I quickly dived under the sheet, even though there wasn't anyone there to see me. Yeah, I had issues, and I was glad Boyd couldn't see. "Okay."

"Okay, you're naked now?"

"Yes. Are you?" How did I get so breathless taking off my pajamas?

I heard the rustle of clothing and the clatter of something metal, maybe his belt buckle hitting the floor. "Gettin' there. Yep, now I am."

My legs swished restlessly under the sheets. "Now what?"

"Do you have any toys, Doctor?"

"Um…" I did. I did have toys. I just hadn't worked up the nerve to use the ones besides the vibrator.

"I can tell by your hesitation the answer's yes. Tell me what you have," he ordered. He was bossy, which I shouldn't like so well, but I did. It was such a different kind of pushy than Jett Markle. I guess because Boyd paid attention to my responses. He listened to what I said. And also to what I didn't say.

"I have a vibrator, standard kind, with an attachment for clitoral stimulation." God, even naked, I sounded like a doctor. "I also got a few things as party favors from an engagement party."

"Sounds like it was a fun party. What did you get?"

"A couple of condoms." Those we gave out at the office the same way a bar handed out matches. That wasn't a big deal to me. But… "A… a vibrating butt plug and lube." I swallowed the last part, like I wasn't sure if I wanted him to hear it or not.

A sound like a growl came through the phone. He didn't make a big deal about it or tease me, which I appreciated. "What's your favorite?" he wondered.

"Well, I ah, haven't used the butt plug yet. I don't know, I guess the time never seemed right."

"You a fan of ass play?"

I was so freaking glad we were on the phone, and he couldn't see my face heating. I even put a hand over my eyes as if that would help share the truth. "Okay, here's the situation." I spoke quickly, as if getting it out faster would make this easier. "I haven't actually tried anal sex, but I'm interested."

Boyd groaned. "I wanna help you with that, darlin'." He sounded pained. "I'm *gonna* help you with that. Tomorrow. *After* I prove I'm interested in more than sex."

"I'm not going to have anal sex with you tomorrow!" I all but shouted. Sure, I'd invited him in with the intention of having sex with him, but anal hadn't even occurred to me. My bottom clenched at the idea. But I shouldn't kid myself, the idea made me wet.

"No, if that ass of yours is virgin, then not tomorrow. But it doesn't mean we won't play. See what you like, how hot it makes you."

I let out a strangled laugh. "Your voice is made to be a phone sex operator."

"Got you all worked up?"

"Uh huh. Maybe you should come tonight." Gawd, I'd never heard my voice sound so husky.

"I'll come, don't you worry none over that. You will, too. My motto is, ladies first."

I rolled my eyes in the dark.

"Get the vibrator—the vaginal one. Turn it on low."

I'd used my vibe before, a bunch of times. But this time was so different. Having Boyd take charge remotely made it sexy times ten. I followed his instructions, switching on the device. It was sleek and pink with an odd shape for internal stimulation as well as external clitoral vibration. It even worked in the shower and had a plug to recharge from a computer.

"Good girl. Now bring it between those pretty thighs. Are you already wet?"

I dragged the vibrator through my juices. "Yes."

He growled again. "Slide your fingers through all that wetness. You doing that?"

"Yes," I breathed, my hips arching up at the contact,

remembering how his thick finger had felt playing with me in his barn.

"Your fingertips all coated with that sticky honey?"

"Yes."

"Good girl. Lick it off."

I stilled but tentatively lifted my fingers to my mouth. My scent was strong, and when I flicked my tongue out, I was mild flavored. Sweet, like he'd said.

"Fuck, I can hear that little tongue at work. I'm picturing it licking up all the pre-cum that's dripping from my dick."

"It is right now?" I asked, licking a little more off my fingertips.

"Like a faucet."

I imagined him being huge. A broad head, thick base. Like a hammer, hard enough to pound nails. It wouldn't be easy to get in me. He'd open me wide, stretch me and fill me to overflowing. I whimpered and clenched down on... nothing.

"Go ahead and slide the vibrator through all that wetness. Then work it in, darlin'."

I obeyed, moaning softly as the toy filled me, then louder when it went deep, and the clit stimulator came into contact with its desired target. It wouldn't be as big as Boyd, but the vibrations were just the right speed, and I'd been primed with a few hours in Boyd's company.

"Oh God," I moaned.

"That's right, darlin'. Does it feel good? Imagine if that was my dick opening you up."

My heart rate increased, and I was panting, undulating my hips under the sheet.

"Now I want to tell you exactly how I'm gonna take care of you and that gorgeous ass of yours. Just close those eyes and feel. 'Cause if you feel this good when we're on the phone, imagine how it's going to be tomorrow once I get my hands on you."

My temperature spiked a few degrees. Boyd Wolf was more than one of the best bull riders in the country. He was also the best dirty-talker. Hands down... or on my pussy.

"First, I'm going to spank that beautiful ass red for being too fucking pretty for me to resist. I'll spank it some more for being a bad girl and letting me get between those lush thighs, getting your flavor all over my tongue and me wild for more."

"Boyd," I gasped, shifting my hand to get the vibrator just right.

Oh! Yes, right there. I'd never had anyone offer to do that before, but it sounded... divine.

"I'm not a bad girl," I said, rolling my hips, realizing no good girl got off with a guy on the phone like this.

"With me you are. That's the way it should be. Your man should see the secret sides of you that you don't show the world. Are your legs parted nice and wide?"

I nodded, but he couldn't see, so I finally gasped a "yes."

"I can picture it, your heels on the bed, knees splayed, that vibrator parting those pink pussy lips of yours and getting in nice and deep. I felt that g-spot, and I bet it's rubbing over it right now."

It was. God, it was.

I arched on the bed, thrusting my breasts up toward the ceiling, my eyes rolling upward with pleasure.

"Then I'm gonna push those knees up and back, spread those cheeks wide and eat your ass. And you may think you won't like it, but you will. I guarantee you that."

Holy. Shit. Not just hot but dirty, too. Filthy dirty. We barely knew each other, and we were going so far past first kisses.

And, no one said he was humble. But I had to say a guy as cocky as Boyd in bed made for a very good time. It eliminated the awkwardness, the waiting for the other person to lead, or not being sure how far to go or what was desired. Nothing was wrong with him. Nothing inappropriate. Nothing shameful. He wasn't modest or afraid of intimacy. He was open, eager to hear what got me hot and wanted to give it to me.

He was cocky, but in this, I was thrilled. I already knew from personal experience he had good reason for his confidence. All I had to do was feel, just like he said.

"Then, when I've got you all worked up back there, I'll see about using that vibrating plug on you. First, I'll dab a little lube on that spit-wet hole and slowly open you up. A little at a time and then trade my finger for that plug. I bet it's a little one too, just right for play. I could even fuck you with it in. Shit, darlin', I'm close to coming."

I was, too. Hanging on his every word, waiting for the *coup de grace* that sent me over the edge. I didn't know what it was going to be, but I knew it was going to be steamier than anything I'd ever read in a romance book.

"I heard that little moan. You want it, don't you? When your ass has taken the plug, that's when I'm gonna stuff your sweet pussy with my cock. And you're going to scream so loud the trees will fall on the mountaintops."

I came. *Hard.* I tried to keep silent, but instead I let out a strangled mewl.

"Fuck, Audrey. Did you just come?" The roughness of Boyd's voice made me come again. It was incredible. More intense than any orgasm I'd ever had, even more potent than the one Boyd had given me in the barn. Then, while I'd let go, I'd held a little back, afraid someone might come in, afraid Boyd might look at my pussy and think it weird looking. *Something.*

But now? This? I'd been completely uninhibited because he had been, too. I could buck and writhe on the vibrator to my wanton heart's content.

"Oh my God. It was... oh, wow."

"Good girl," he growled.

I huffed out a little laugh although I had no energy to barely do that. "I thought you said I was a bad girl."

"You're both. For me."

I smiled into the darkness. I felt relaxed, sated. Sleepy.

I wanted to return the favor—tell Boyd how I'd put my lips over the head of his cock and suck hard until he came, but I was still breathless when I heard him groan, too.

"Did you?" I finally managed to say. I switched off the vibrator and slid it out and dropped it onto the bed

"Fuck, darlin'. I came like a fucking freight train. Cum's all over the place. And that's just from me *picturing* you coming. I can't wait until I see the real deal again. Feel the way your pussy's going to squeeze my dick when you come. Drip all over it."

The release made me bold, and his words made me return to reality. I couldn't wrap my head around all this attention this guy was pouring on me. "I still don't get it, Boyd. Why me?"

He growled, this time, not in pleasure. "There are other reasons why I might toss you over my knee and spank you, and putting yourself down is on top of that list."

"Boyd," I said, as if that would explain everything.

"Do you believe in fate?"

I frowned. "No. I'm a scientist. We believe in evidence-based reasoning."

"You also said every baby was a miracle."

My stomach flopped a little. He'd listened. This guy really listened to me. "Well, yeah. You got me there. But that's the miracle of nature."

"The way my body reacts to yours is also a miracle of nature."

I laughed because he was right. The physical response I had to him, my nipples hardening, my body heating, my pussy getting wet, was all a body's way of ensuring procreation. It wasn't romantic or sexy. It was a fact. I was biologically attracted to him, so I could birth his babies.

I envisioned little boys looking just like Boyd, and it was possible my ovary just popped out an egg.

"Okay, I get what you're saying."

"I want more than your body," he amended quickly, like he just realized he made a mistake. "Doc, you're smart, caring, kind. You love babies. You're beautiful."

"I don't know about that."

"You're *beautiful.* I'm not sure why you don't see it. Don't worry, I'll get you to believe it soon enough."

"You're telling me you're interested in settling down in Cooper Valley. Raising kids? Because car seats don't fit on the back of a bull."

My voice raised on the last word. I shouldn't be afraid to make it very clear what I wanted, what I wouldn't compromise.

"I've worked too hard for too long to get where I am to settle."

"You shouldn't fucking settle, ever," he all but growled.

"Boyd, you've worked really hard for your championships. You shouldn't have to settle either. I just don't see how it could work."

"Now hold on," he prompted. "I've admitted I've had

some wild ways. You dated Jett Markle before me. You dated until you met me."

"I didn't sleep with him or pretty much all the other dates I've had."

"Darlin', you keep bringing up my past. Do you really want to talk about who I've had sex with?"

I pursed my lips. "No."

"While I don't like to think about any guy touching you, what you did before we met is in the past. Same goes for me. It's what we do with the now, together, that matters. I'm telling you I'm all in. You. Kids. A dog. The whole deal. Do I have to grab you by the hair and drag you back to my cave for you to believe it?"

I couldn't help but laugh at the image he painted.

"No." I sighed, then took a leap. "Okay."

"Okay?"

"Yes. Okay."

"Okay, you'll mate—I mean marry me—and have my children?"

I laughed. "Okay, I'll go on a date with you tomorrow."

"That's a good fucking start. I can live with that."

I stifled a yawn, and he heard it. "You need some sleep, Doc. Think you can rest now that your pussy's all taken care of?"

"Yes," I said softly. "Thank you."

"For helping you get off? Trust me, it was my pleasure. Hearing you come is at the top of my list for bedtime activities. Good night, Audrey."

"Night."

15

Boyd

I swung off Chesapeake, my mare, to examine a break in the fence line. I'd ridden out to the back range, where the pasture met the mountains, the sun just breaking over the sharp peaks in the distance. The view was incredible, and I thought of what Audrey had said. This was the most perfect place. It was an incredible summer day. It was warming up quick, but a light breeze would keep it from getting blistering. The smell of fresh grass and pine filled the air.

Sure, I traveled to great places all over the country and up into Canada, but I hadn't realized how much I'd missed it here. How much I'd taken *home* for granted. I remembered what it had been like before my parents died. The carefree way my brothers and I had roamed the land, and that had been before any of us could shift. But others had. We'd have bonfires or even ice skating parties, and the elders would shift and run.

I'd felt awe and envy at the ability to turn into their wolf and go. Rob, then Colton, had begun to shift, and while we'd been close, they'd been able to join in on the fun I'd missed. In fact, I'd never once been able to participate because the first time I shifted, it had been because of the stress of the accident, the need to survive. My wolf had saved me. My parents, though, had died. So had all the fun. We'd still remained a pack, but the heart had left it.

Scanning the land, it hadn't changed in the almost two decades since they died. The mountains were as tall as ever, the snow still capped the peaks. Birds still caught the wind. The river still flowed. It would in another twenty years. Thirty. Fifty. What mattered was a strong pack to carry it on. I'd never once felt the desire to do so. Until now. Until Audrey.

I could see pups of our own who'd tumble and play and ultimately shift and run. I wanted to do it with them. To pass on the joy of the land. Perhaps this was my shot.

It had to be Audrey, but I had to figure out how. The question of how to mate her would never go away. I had to solve it. A falcon soared overhead and stirred me from my thoughts.

It was mid-morning, and I was on my own because Rob and the ranch hands had ridden out without me. That's what I got for waking up late.

For once, it didn't bother me a bit. I didn't feel like a failure or that I'd disappointed my big brother. Nope. I was on top of the world. Jerking off to the sultry sounds of Audrey using a vibrator had been better than any sexual encounter I'd had before. Besides getting my mouth on her sweet pussy in the barn. *That* had been heaven although I hadn't gotten off. Maybe that was why I'd come so hard the night before. I'd had all that need, all that cum built up.

I couldn't wait for our hot date. I'd spend the day out here in the wilderness, so I didn't get in my truck and head to the maternity floor and wait for her.

Yeah, I'd lost it. Maybe I had hit my head when I'd been bucked from the bull. I grinned. I didn't give a shit. I was loving being not right in the head. She was addictive. I'd spent last night in her company, and I couldn't wait to see her again. Any woman before her, and I'd have forgotten her name by now. They'd been fun but not memorable. Not worthy of being my mate. Audrey was.

I pulled the tools from my saddle bag and began to repair the break in the fence. It was sweaty, manual work, but it felt good. As I finished, a scent made me pause. I lifted my head, took in the direction of the wind, where it was coming from.

Wolf shifter, but not one I recognized. Not one of the ranch hands or Rob.

And no other wolf should be on our property.

Of course, Rob could've held a pack meeting down at the ranch that I didn't know about.

Except that didn't make sense. He never would call attention to the pack that way. We always met up at a cabin in the mountains. One where wolves could run without fear of being spotted by humans. While he might think of me as a fuck up, he'd have told me about a meeting.

So if I was catching the scent of a strange shifter here at the fenceline, maybe Markle was right. There was a wolf around. Still, I refused to believe it had taken down any of his cattle. No shifter would do such a thing.

With the repair finished, I put my tools away and headed down the hill. I'd tell Rob about what I'd discovered. Twenty minutes later, I dismounted and led Chesapeake to the stable where I could brush her down.

I didn't have to go find Rob because he was waiting for me, like he wanted to catch me out of earshot of the rest of the guys.

"I heard you caused a scene with Markle and the doctor last night. What in the hell is going on?" He paced the hard-packed ground.

I took the hat from my head, hooked it over one of the posts. The back of my neck got hot and prickly, and I rubbed it.

"They went out on one date. Didn't go well. Markle's been harassing her. Wouldn't take no for an answer. The guy's a real asshole."

Rob's eyes narrowed. "Well, that's just not right."

He didn't like a guy fucking with a woman any more than I did. He might be a prickly fucker, but he wouldn't stand for that kind of shit. We stood up for those weaker than us. While Audrey outsmarted the pants off me and could take care of herself, she was smaller than a guy like Markle and an asshole could overpower her easily enough.

"Fine, you protected her. I won't argue with that. The thing is, I sent you down there to smooth talk the guy and instead you caused more friction."

I didn't usually give my brother shit back. Staying away was usually the way I handled myself when it came to dealing with family tension. But today, I had no patience. "Smooth talk? Kinda like you did when he showed up here wanting to organize a wolf hunt?"

Rob took his hat off and slapped it against his leg. He looked down at the ground and seemed to be more pissed about the situation than me. "I know. Hell, the man's lucky I didn't shove my boot up his ass. But you got all the charm in the family. You're supposed to smooth over my social fuckups."

Huh. Was that actually a compliment? From my big brother? Would wonders ever cease?

"Yeah, well, my charm evaporated pretty quick when I found out he'd been harassing my—" I stopped myself before I said *mate*. "—doctor."

Rob nodded. "Can't blame you for that."

"Really, 'cause it kinda seemed like you just did." As I said, I didn't usually give Rob shit, especially because he was alpha, but something made me push back today.

Audrey.

She was worth fighting for, even with my brother. I wanted him to know I wasn't going to take any kind of shit talk about her.

Rob put his hat back on his head and walked out of the barn, shaking his head. When he got to the open doorway, he turned. "All I want to hear is that you've fixed it. The problem with the doctor and the problem with our neighbor. Can you do that for me?"

He was looking at me with his usual dark, focused gaze. He wasn't fucking with me. He was entrusting these pack problems to me. One was my doing, the other bad luck that Markle had bought the property down the road. Rob wanted me to solve them. He wasn't micromanaging or whatever the fucking term was. Did it mean he trusted me or that I was good at dealing with messes?

I was tempted to refuse because me making nice with Jett Markle wasn't going to happen now. Not after the line I drew in the sand with him the night before. Especially when Audrey had used me to get him off her back. As if I'd play nice with a guy who was a dick to women.

Instead, I nodded and said, "I'll do my best."

Because he was the alpha, and respect for the alpha was in our bones. And, my need to please my big brother, to make him proud of me, to make me worthy of being in the pack even though I'd single-handedly destroyed it, was still something I craved.

It wasn't until he walked away that I remembered the wolf scent. I'd tell him about that later because right now, I had to clean up for my date. I had a different scent on my mind now: juicy, sweet peaches.

16

Audrey

"Where are we going?" I asked for the third time. We were in Boyd's truck, driving in the direction of his ranch. Work had gone by impossibly slow this morning because all I could think about was our date. I'd called Marina to catch her up on the latest although I'd left the details out about the wild time in the barn. That was a secret for me and Boyd. And anyone else at the Wolf Ranch who'd heard me scream as I came. Instead, I'd told her about the run-in with Jett Markle, the mechanical bull and how Boyd had followed me home. I'd also left out the phone sex. That was why she was more eager than ever for me to get my rocks off with Boyd, even if he wasn't future husband material.

I still had my doubts, even after everything he'd said on the phone about love at first sight, but I was willing to explore this insane and apparently mutual attraction a little further. It seemed I was a glutton for punishment. And orgasms.

He flicked his gaze my way and grinned. "I'm taking you to one of Cooper Valley's best kept secrets. One of nature's most beautiful features that you won't find in any guide book."

"And we need the butt plug for that?"

When Boyd picked me up, he'd insisted I bring the party favors. Lube, condoms, vibrating butt plug. When I'd stared at him by the front door, he'd stormed past, into my bedroom and found my bedside drawer that had them. I was eager and apprehensive to think about what we'd do with them. I knew the plug would go in my butt—I didn't think Boyd was game for the other way around—and I vividly remembered his intentions. That made me squirm on his leather seat.

The corner of his mouth tipped up as if he'd caught me. "Well, I brought some blankets in case we wanted to pick up where we left off last night." He tossed one of those Boyd Wolf signature winks my way, and my panties got damp. Blankets meant not in a bed. He was planning on plugging my ass and fucking me *outside?*

Yes, I did want to pick up where we left off last night. In fact, I'd struggled to think of anything else since.

That wasn't true. I'd thought a lot about the phone sex, but I'd also thought about earlier at the bar. How quickly Boyd went with it when I suddenly one-eightied on him and pretended he was my boyfriend. The sweet way he got me on that mechanical bull. How he'd been concerned about me getting enough sleep before I had to work. How he'd followed me home.

I'd underestimated Boyd. Grossly. And I may have underestimated his sexual fantasies. I wasn't a virgin, but could I keep up with a guy like Boyd? My pussy told me it wanted to try.

A pang of guilt settled in my chest. Here I'd thought him shallow, a quick lay, when in fact, I'd been pigeon-holing him. He was the real deal. A protective, thoughtful guy in a crazy-hot cowboy package. Who wanted to play with me using a butt plug. As Marina had said, *go for it*.

I couldn't freaking wait.

"Did you always want to be a doctor?" he asked, completely changing the subject. He glanced my way, then flicked on his blinker and turned down a side road. We'd cut through the canyon and were about a mile from Wolf Ranch. The turn meant we weren't heading there, though.

"Pretty much. My mom was... well, sickly."

"Bad heart or something?"

In a way, it was true. "That's what they called it back then. *Sickly*. In medical terms, she was clinically depressed. She'd sleep a lot although she worked two jobs, so she was tired all the time. She didn't have hobbies or socialize. Sometimes she'd forget to eat, and I'd have to find food and cook for us both."

I saw his fingers tighten on the steering wheel.

"Didn't your dad help?"

I bit my lip, stared out the side window. "I never knew my dad. At least not when I was a kid. My mom got pregnant when she was eighteen and told me she never knew his name."

It made no sense now. I was thirty, her age when I'd been twelve. I remember being twelve, and her answer about my father had confused me. I'd known the basics about sex at the time and could never understand how she didn't know who my dad was.

"She killed herself when I was in college. Looking back,

I think my dad screwed her over, or she thought he did. Maybe it was a quick fling or a teenaged one-night stand. Whatever it was, it didn't have the outcome she'd expected. People who have mental illness can often have some kind of snap, and I think that happened when she got pregnant with me. It's possible, or most likely, her sick mind distorted what really happened over time."

He slowed the truck and pulled over to the side of the road. It was a dirt backroad, and no one else was around. I turned to look at him as he shifted to face me, his forearm resting on the steering wheel. "You can't believe it was your fault. Her death."

I shook my head. "No, not at all. I just never knew her when she wasn't depressed."

"Obviously, you went to college, then medical school."

I licked my lips and couldn't look away from his piercing eyes. He wanted to know this, not only the good stuff, the fun stuff like butt plugs and phone sex, but the messy stuff like my family life.

"Being at home wasn't all that great. Don't get me wrong, I had friends and sleepovers and prom and stuff, but I pretty much hunkered down in my room. Studying was easy. I could get lost in it. I knew it was my way out. I got a full ride for undergrad, and I got loans for med school. That's why I filled in at the arena. Extra cash pays off med school faster."

"Why didn't you go into mental health?"

I huffed out a laugh. "I grew up in it. Knew it wasn't for me. Babies. That was my focus all along. If you analyzed me, you'd say I'm seeking to make a family because it was absent from my childhood."

His gaze raked over me before he spoke. "There's no shame in wanting a family. In wanting babies. Children.

Homework. Sticky stuff on the floor you have no idea what it is. A tire swing. Children who know they're loved."

My chest ached with the desire for everything he said. I did want all of that, as if he'd made a checklist of things I envisioned my family being like. It sounded as if he knew what that was like.

"Is that how it was for you? Two parents you knew loved you? A tire swing?"

"Yeah, I had all that. Until I was twelve. I was lucky. I have Rob and Colton. You didn't have any siblings to grow up with. To fight and bicker with. Annoy."

I raised my hand, waved it in the air. "Actually, I have a half sister. Marina. She's twenty-one. I only learned she existed two years ago. She did the DNA testing and found we were a match."

"She's not your mom's."

Shaking my head, I continued. "No, my dad. He was young, nineteen, when he had sex with my mom. He never knew about me. He married at twenty-eight and had Marina with his wife."

"He didn't tell you what happened?"

I pushed my glasses up my nose. "I don't want to know. Would you want to know about how you were conceived?"

He looked horrified. "I see your point."

"I'm not close with him. I've met him. I look like him. They live in southern California. I did my residency in Chicago. Our paths don't cross."

"But your sister?"

I couldn't help but smile when thinking of Marina. "She's great. Sweet. Definitely a little wilder than I am. We talk all the time. She's in college for engineering. I'm... I'm glad I have her."

He eyed me for a moment, then gave me a nod and put the truck in gear and back on our way.

We were quiet for a minute. "Boyd..." I bit my lip, knowing that I was asking a question that might upset him. "Um... what happened when you were twelve?"

He cleared his throat, clenched the steering wheel. "I guess it's best you find out now. I've been clear from the start how much I want you. It's pretty obvious I'm just a dumb jock, that you're way outta my league. I was hoping maybe you could look past that, but this might change your mind about me."

I frowned, felt apprehension and worry lodge in my belly.

"When I was twelve, I killed my parents."

17

Audrey

I stared at him as he turned onto a narrow road. I wondered if it was someone's property or a service access for the National Forest. Either way, there was no one around for miles. His words had stunned me into silence and made me think all kinds of things. Murder? Had he run over them with a tractor?

"What do you mean you killed your parents?" I finally asked. With my window open, the breeze caught on my hair, and I tucked it back behind my ear.

He didn't look my way, just stayed quiet and focused on the rutted road.

"Boyd," I prompted, setting my hand on his thigh. The muscle clenched beneath my fingers, and I tried to move my hand away, but he grabbed it, pressed it back in place. He didn't let go.

"I'm not talking about this in the truck. They've been

gone for a long time. It won't change in the next few minutes."

That was true, so I gave him the room he seemed to really want and stayed silent. Within five minutes, he pulled over and parked. Where he stopped looked like where we'd been since we turned off the main road and the next half mile in front of us. We were close to the mountains, but still in the rolling grassland. Pines dotted the craggy rocks in the distance, but it was a golden grassy carpet that surrounded us.

"We're here. Come on."

He opened his door and hopped down. I watched as he came around the front in my direction. I got out, and he pushed my door shut behind me. With his big hand, he stroked my hair. "I'll tell you now because I want to leave it here by the truck. I want our time at the spot to be special, not tainted with what I did."

I licked my lips, suddenly nervous. If I'd read him wrong all along, I was out in the middle of nowhere. "Please don't tell me you're an ax murderer or serial killer or something."

One pale brow winged up.

"My parents were killed in a car accident. A rock slide washed our truck off the road. They were killed instantly. I survived in the back seat."

My heart ached for him trying to imagine what it had been like to survive something like that. I blinked back the instant tears.

"Then why—"

"I'm not like my brothers. I wasn't then, and I'm not now. I wanted off the ranch and to hang with my friends at the fair." He told me about a barfing contest and how he'd been late for the agreed upon pick up time. "If I'd shown up when I was supposed to, we'd have been ahead of the storm."

I set my hand on his arm, squeezed. His muscle was like a rock without any give. So strong, but yet he revealed how fragile he was. How damaged.

"Boyd, it's not your fault."

"I'd been too eager to see Bobby Sweetin hurl."

"You were twelve. That's what boys that age like to do. They're gross and a little selfish."

"Not every middle schooler has their selfish actions kill their parents," he countered.

"The rock slide killed them. When you finally showed up, were they mad?"

He looked into the distance, as if not seeing the mountains, but into the past. "No. They were standing by the front of the car talking with friends of theirs."

"So they were fine staying at the fair longer. Maybe if you'd shown up on time, they'd have remained and chatted anyway."

Frowning, he remained quiet.

"You'll have to tell me about them sometime. They'd be proud of you, knowing all you've accomplished. They'd be honored that you cared for them so much you took on this burden of their deaths. But they wouldn't want you to carry that."

His gaze dropped to mine.

"Would they?" I asked.

He hesitated, then shook his head. There was nothing more to say about the topic for now. He'd been living with it for so long, he'd need to think. To process.

"Where's this special spot you were telling me about?"

Relief washed over his face. His muscles relaxed, and the corner of his mouth tipped up. "I'll grab the blankets and the food from the back. You grab those toys of yours."

Just like that, the easygoing Boyd was back. But I'd seen

a side of him he probably hadn't even shown his brothers. That meant things were deep. Real deep.

I opened the cab door and leaned in, grabbed the plug and lube he'd pulled from my bedside drawer. Speaking of deep. I clenched my bottom in anticipation of what was to come.

BOYD

After grabbing the blanket and basket, I raised the tailgate back into place. Talking about my parents stirred shit up. Anger. Shame. Guilt. It never went away, but after all this time, I'd gotten pretty damned good at pushing it down and covering it up with wit and cockiness. Unfortunately, Audrey had seen right through all of that from the very beginning.

It's not your fault.

She'd said exactly what I thought was a lie. She'd also put doubt in my mind. Had I been living with the guilt of a twelve-year-old? Had I been seeing it from a kid's perspective all this time? I'd waited for my rodeo buddies often enough. People showed up late for shit all the time. Yet no one had been killed in a car accident right after.

I'd forgotten that my parents had been talking with the Gundersons when I ran up to the car. Mom had wrapped an arm around me and squeezed me. Dad had ruffled my hair, and I'd climbed into the back to wait. They'd continued to talk for another five or ten minutes. I remembered now because I'd stuck my head out the window to tell them I had to pee, and I'd even run off to the restroom while they finished their conversation.

Shit, I'd forgotten all about that. I blinked, stared at the back of my truck. Yeah, I'd been late. But that wasn't the only reason we'd ended up in the canyon when the storm came through. I'd have to think on it, about everything. I'd been so bent out of shape over it—and rightly so—but I wasn't the only one with a fucked-up childhood. With bad stuff happening to them.

Audrey hadn't had an easy time. Parents were supposed to take care of their kids, not the other way around. At least Mom and Dad had never once made me think I wasn't loved or wanted. I'd been lucky, even though they'd died. I had a lot to think about.

But not now. The sun was shining. The spring-fed pool was just over the hill. And I had the best companion ever. My fucking *mate*. Soon enough, she'd also be my *fucking* mate.

I adjusted myself, went around the truck and halted in my tracks.

Audrey was leaning into the cab. Since she was so short, she was up on her toes and her ass stuck out.

Fuck. Me.

In her snug jeans and tank top, I couldn't miss every inch of her curves. I'd had my hands on them the other day, knew the width of her hips as I held her in place for my tongue and fingers. My mouth watered with the need to get back there and taste her some more. It was her tits, small lush swells pressing against the pale blue stretchy fabric, that I hadn't seen. Touched. Tasted. Licked. Sucked.

She dropped down to the soles of her feet.

"Hold it right there."

She froze facing the interior of the truck but turned her

head to look at me. Her eyes instantly widened, and I couldn't miss the way her pupils dilated behind her glasses. I felt more wolf than human at the moment. Her scent caught the air, and I breathed it in. Sweetness, but also musk. Fuck, she was wet. Just as eager for me as I was for her. The last thing I'd said was for her to get the butt plug and lube, which meant—

I set the blankets over the side of the truck bed and placed the food basket on the ground.

"What?" she asked.

"I want to mark you." My voice was deep. Rough. I was barely hanging on. Maybe it was the talk about my parents. Or her parents. Or the fact that we'd shared shit that I never told anyone. Rob didn't know I blamed myself. I knew *he* blamed me, but I'd never outright said it was my fault. I'd never apologized to him for making him alpha when he wasn't ready.

Something was different, though. Inside, I felt lighter. I wasn't absolved, but Audrey hadn't slapped me and jumped from the truck. She hadn't rejected me. In fact, she'd told me I wasn't to blame.

Someone liked me, wanted me, was staying with me even with all my fuck ups. Somehow, she'd seen every bit of my false bravado, the cockiness for what it was. She'd heard my darkest secrets, and she was dripping wet for me.

She was mine. Not just mine as in bend her over and fuck her. No, as in, I loved her. She was my other half. I didn't give a shit if she was human. I couldn't bite her, but I could mark her in other ways. My cum on her skin, dripping from her pussy. My scent on her so every wolf in the west knew she'd been claimed, that could come later. But right this second, I needed to see my mark on her.

I stepped up behind her within the open door, reached

around and undid the front of her jeans, pushed them over her hips. She held still for me, almost shaking with anticipation. Her gorgeous ass was covered in red satin. Fuck, that was hot, and I'd get those off her later, but now I needed her ass bare. I needed all that creamy skin on display. So I could mark.

Hooking my fingers in her panties, I lowered them, so they and her jeans were bunched mid-thigh. I heard her ragged breathing, saw the frantic beat of her pulse at her neck.

"Boyd." Her voice was almost a whisper, but I heard it as if she'd shouted.

My hand slid over her ass, caressed it. Cupped it. Squeezed it.

"Can you tell I'm an ass man?"

She laughed, but she was too aroused and stopped as soon as I lifted my hand and spanked her. Not too hard, but the crack resounded through the air.

She gasped, bucked, but held herself still, ready for more. Just as I'd thought. She liked it. The air around us practically crackled with sexual electricity. My dick punched against my jeans to get out. I slapped her ass again and watched as her flesh jiggled. Instantly, another handprint bloomed pink.

"Marked." I spanked her again. Again. Switching sides, I lit up her skin. This wasn't a punishment, and I kept things light, but she was no doubt feeling a hot ass right now. She wiggled her hips, thrust her hips out more.

Tapping the inside of one thigh, I nudged her feet apart, but she could only go so far with her jeans about her thighs. Still, the extra few inches put her pussy on display. She didn't wax herself bare. Her labia had trimmed dark hair that only accentuated how pink her inner lips were. And wet. She was soaked.

I must have stared too long because she whimpered, then called my name.

"What is it, darlin'? Need to come 'cause you're getting your ass spanked?"

"I've... it's... yes!"

I cupped her heated skin, stroked it. "Never been spanked before?"

She shook her head, her hair falling down over her shoulders.

"We're going to find out all the things you like. Every." I spanked her. "Single." Again. "One."

Her moan caught the air.

"Hand me that plug."

She'd been holding it in her hand this whole time.

"Boyd," she whispered again.

I leaned over her, my front pressed to her back, whispered in her ear. "You can say no. I'll pull up your panties and jeans, and we'll go to the watering hole right now, darlin'. You tell me what you want."

"I... I'm not sure."

She shivered, and I kissed her ear, along the side of her neck.

"Do you want to come?"

She nodded.

"Gotta hear you say it."

"Yes."

"Do you trust me?"

She didn't pause. Didn't even blink. "Yes."

"Ah, my sweet, sweet darlin'."

Then I spanked her again.

"So sweet and *so* bad."

I took the plug from her hold and stood back up. The

plug was small, about the size of my thumb, with a narrow tip, a wider section in the middle and a base that I knew would fit snug between her cheeks. And it vibrated.

Perfect.

While it was made of silicone and smooth to the touch, it had only a little bit of give and was sturdy enough to work into her. I slid it back and forth over her heated cheeks, letting her get used to the feel of it. With my other hand, I cupped her pussy and instantly my fingers were coated. Even though I got her verbal consent, she wasn't lying about her desire. She wasn't giving in for the sake of pleasing the rodeo champ.

I made her hot. Wet. Eager to come.

How could I refuse? I had to go slow though, to take my time. No matter how much I wanted to get my fingers inside her, feel how tight and hot she was, it was the one place I didn't go. Getting in her ass required her to be so worked up she was losing her mind and that was one way to do it.

Not long, she began to roll her hips, tried to get my fingers to go where she wanted them. I spanked her again, my sticky fingers leaving a wet spot on her pink ass. "Nope, darlin'. Who's in charge here?"

"You are."

"That's right." Setting my hand at the base of her spine, I used my thumb to part her pert cheeks and fuck, found her tight little hole. It winked at me and knew she was eager for it.

"Hurry," she whined.

I couldn't help but grin. When she got going, she didn't hold back.

I slid the toy through her sticky honey, got it all coated, but still grabbed the sample sized bottle of lube and flipped the top with my thumb. With a gentle squeeze, I dribbled a few drops onto her hole.

She gasped, then stilled. I circled the tip of the plug through the lube, coating the tip, getting her used to something touching the outside of her anus. Her fingers clenched the truck seat and she jolted.

"Shh." I soothed her like I would a skittish mare. Gently pressing, I nudged the tip of the plug into her, but just the very tip, then pulled back. Again and again, I did that, getting a little bit more into her until she was pushing back and working the plug in herself.

"That's it, darlin'. Take it nice and deep." In one careful push, I got the broadest part into her, and then it popped into place, her muscles tightening back around it.

"Fuck me, ain't you a sight."

"Boyd," she practically growled, making me wonder if she wasn't part wolf.

I couldn't stand around and admire how pretty she was, pussy glistening and a plug in her ass. She'd been a good girl and she deserved a reward. My fingers in her pussy. I worked into her, then another and curled them over her g-spot.

"Yes!" she cried.

"Get ready, darlin'. Brace yourself." I pressed the button on the plug and the vibrations kicked in.

Instantly, her inner walls clamped down on my fingers.

"Oh my God," she groaned. "Boyd... it's... I'm going to come."

Not two seconds after the vibrations began, she did just that. Her head went back, her hair flying over her back like a wild stallion's. She screamed. A blood curdling cry as if she'd had no idea an orgasm like that could happen. Her pussy milked my fingers, dripped her cream.

Sweat bloomed on her pink ass as she tried to catch her breath.

It was the most beautiful thing I ever saw.

I slowed my fingers, just kept them inside her as she came down from the orgasm that seemed to go on and on. When she slumped against the seat, I turned off the plug, stroked the smooth skin of her ass.

"One of these days, we're going to get you naked. I want to see all of you, get my hands on those beautiful tits."

I heard her laugh, and she pushed herself up. I stepped back enough, so she could turn around and face me, her pants still down. She had a sloppy smile on her face, her cheeks were flushed, and her eyes were all blurry behind her glasses.

"Did you know we've barely kissed?"

I looked at her lips and realized she was right. I hadn't sampled them enough. I was about to lower my head and take her mouth, but her hand wrapped around my neck and tugged me down. She was aggressive, and I liked it.

Her tongue found mine, and I had no idea how long we stood there and just kissed. My dick was going to have a zipper mark and my balls were probably going to fall off, but I was happy.

Finally, I lifted my head. "Come on, let's get that plug out and fix your pants. I got distracted, and we still haven't made it to the secret spot."

She gripped my shirt, not allowing me to step back. "What about you?" She looked down at my crotch, and I almost came in my pants. She could no doubt see the pre-cum stain on my jeans as it was seeping non-stop. Her hand slid down my chest and cupped me. I hissed and closed my eyes at the feel.

"Later. Let's get to the spot first."

When she didn't move her hand away but cupped me more firmly, I looked down at her. "Audrey."

"Here. Now. You've gotten me off three times, and all you've done is come in your hand."

"At the watering hole."

"Here." Slowly, she turned back around and bent over like she had been, offering up her pussy with her ass still plugged.

Fuck. Me.

My wolf said now. My dick said now.

Fine. Now.

"Here, but I want to see you."

With my hands on her hips, I picked her up and carried her to the back of the truck, grabbing a blanket on the way. I set her down long enough to drop the tailgate, toss the blanket down, then pick her up and set her upon it. "Lean back."

She did as I told her, so she wasn't sitting directly on the plug. I tugged off her shoes, then got her jeans and panties down her legs in seconds, so she was bare from the waist down, her feet dangling off the edge. That wasn't enough. I needed all of her.

"Shirt off."

She worked the tank top over her head and didn't linger before unhooking the back of her bra and dropping it beside her.

"Holy shit, woman. You're gorgeous."

"I'm short and curvy."

My gaze raked over every perfect inch of her. "Yes, you are. Just the way I like."

She blushed. After everything we'd just done, she blushed.

Taking one ankle in hand, I set her foot on the very edge of the tailgate, then the other.

She lowered herself to the blanket as I pushed her knees wide. Her pussy was right there at the edge of the tailgate and it was at exactly the right height to fuck.

Opening my jeans, I pulled out my dick, sheathed it in a condom I pulled from my shirt pocket.

She looked at my dick, her eyes widening. "Wow."

I grinned and looked down her lush body. "Wow is right."

"Now," she all but begged. I didn't need to be told twice, and I stepped close, gripped the base of my dick and slid the tip through her slick folds. I loved the sight of her, all eager and wet, her ass filled.

I didn't wait. I couldn't. I'd been hard for her since I first saw her. In one stroke, I slid deep, parting her pink lips and opening her wide. Slapping my hands on the truck bed beside her head, I held myself deep.

She looked up at me, her eyes wide, her lips parted.

"Boyd, move, please."

I grinned, then gave her what she wanted. Slow in and out strokes that made my wolf howl. She was so tight, so hot, even through the latex barrier. I wanted to pull out, yank it off and take her bare. Not yet. Soon.

Now, I claimed, let her see what it would be like between us. I could feel the firmness of the plug as it stroked the bottom side of my dick. The combination of Audrey's tight sheath and the hard feel of the toy pushed me to the brink. It was too good.

I was going to come, but not before she did.

"Again," I growled. She arched her hips up to meet me. My balls slapped against the base of the plug. The scent of fucking, of her sweet musk, filled my nostrils.

Mine. She was mine. On the back of my truck. No soft bed. No sweet words. Just hard fucking with a plug in her ass.

And she loved it.

I slipped my hand between us and flicked her clit with my thumb. Leaning down, took a taut nipple into my mouth. Sucked.

Fuck yes.

"Boyd!" she cried, fucking me as much as I was fucking her. Her inner walls clenched, and she tugged on my hair. She was going to come, and my wolf was thrilled with our prowess. We could sexually satisfy our woman.

She came, but there was no scream this time, only gasps as she milked my dick. I didn't last. I couldn't. I didn't want to. I didn't even care that I'd come in under two minutes. I'd take her again as planned by the watering hole. In my bed later. But I'd come now, satisfy her, myself and my wolf.

My balls tightened, my dick thickened, and I thrust deep, held still as I shook with the ferocity of my orgasm. I lifted my head as I growled, afraid I'd bite her breast.

We were a sweaty mess when we both recovered, but I didn't pull out. Not yet. I stroked her hair back, kissed her. Gently. Sweetly.

"Okay?" I murmured.

She nodded. "Again."

Slowly, I smiled. "You're a greedy little thing, aren't you?"

My dick started to swell, and I had to pull out, carefully holding the condom.

"Kinky, too."

"Yeah, I guess I am. With you."

I growled. "That's right. Only with me."

I took care of the condom, then the butt plug. "Come on,

darlin'. Let's get to the watering hole as I wanted. Then you can have your way with me."

I winked and helped her back in her clothes. I wanted her to remain bare, to walk naked as I often did after a shift and a run. She didn't need clothes here, not with me. Not with anyone around.

I'd get her there. For now, I'd get her to the secret spot, get her naked again. She liked it wild, she liked it rough. I'd give her anything she wanted. *Do* anything she wanted. Ensure she knew she was mine. When I helped her down from the truck bed and saw her reddened ass, I knew she already was.

18

Audrey

Everything tingled. My ass, my clit, my nipples. My lips. And the oxytocin—what we'd called *the love hormone* in med school—plowing through my system had me soaring. Bonding.

I was definitely feeling the love.

In all kinds of ways.

It was more than physical, and that part scared the hell out of me. Marina had told me to climb Boyd like a tree. Becky, who'd never met my sister, would high five her and agree. I'd wanted to get laid, get some man-made orgasms and have a little fun.

Check and check.

I hadn't expected Boyd to turn out to be so much more than I gave him credit for. He was almost too good to be true. Cocky, sure. He'd proven he was a skilled lover. No wonder women eyed him like he was the last piece of chocolate in a box. I craved him now.

I guess that made me nervous. Because I'd learned if something seemed too good to be true, it usually was.

I wasn't going to give any attention to my fears right now, though. The day was gorgeous, and my body thrummed with pleasure. I was following Boyd across the field. His long legs ate up the distance, and I couldn't keep up. He slowed, held out his hand, and I took it. He didn't let go as he led me to—

"Is that water?" I asked as we headed down a barely-there narrow footpath. I assumed we were on private property, but the place was visited enough to have a worn-down area in the grass. We were about ten minutes from the truck and had gone higher and close to the mountains. Small boulders dotted the hillside, scraggly bushes and even a cottonwood or two offered dappled spots of shade. I stopped short and gasped when we rounded a corner. "Oh my God, Boyd. This is incredible."

In front of us, a small, fifteen-foot waterfall dazzled, dropping freely over a moss-covered rock lip to feed what appeared to be a deep pool.

He looked my way and grinned. "I know, darlin'. It's private property, Old Man Shefield's land. Wolf Ranch is his next-door neighbor, so I've been coming here since I was a tot. He died a few months ago, sadly."

I turned around and looked east. I couldn't see the house for this property or any of the buildings on Wolf Ranch. He leaned close and pointed over my shoulder.

"Wolf Ranch is that way."

"This is one of those things you did as a kid? Roamed free and got to come up here with your brothers?"

I turned back around, took in the water. It would be

called a pond because of the size. It was perhaps only thirty feet across. Excess water escaped over the bank and made a little stream that went down the hillside.

"Sure did."

I could envision Boyd as a boy, pale tousled hair and gangly arms and legs, running after his older brothers and splashing in the water. It had to have been such a carefree childhood. Until—

"Do you swim here?" I asked, steering my thoughts away from what had happened to his parents. I wondered if he came here much after their deaths.

"Yes. Feel the water. You won't believe it."

I walked to the water's edge, squatted down and stuck my fingertips in. "It's so warm! Is it a hot spring?"

He nodded, then tipped his chin. "Yep. The waterfall is runoff and cold as hell. Beneath it, coming out of the ground is a spring. Water's really hot, so careful if you go in that corner. It all mixes together to make it just right. I've even come here in the winter."

I looked up at him, wondering if he was teasing me. There were hot springs all over the west and in this area, the same underground source that fed Yellowstone's hot springs and geysers. Most were public and made into baths, but this...

A private oasis.

I dipped my fingertips in. The water was perfect, like a tepid bath. "This is incredible!" I shouted.

Boyd chuckled. "I know it is. Aren't you glad you finally agreed to let me show you around?"

Yes. For more reasons than one. I just hadn't expected a tour like this.

I started stripping off my clothes. "Last one in is a rotten egg!"

Boyd whooped and tore off his jeans and t-shirt. I stopped to admire him as I'd yet to see him naked. My eye was drawn to the white bandage over the place he'd been gored. I would've sworn it was a little lower below his ribs, but I must've remembered wrong, just like how injured he'd really been.

Despite my doctorly concern, my attention shifted to his exquisite body. The guy was perfect. His shoulders were broad, his chest muscle-packed and hairy—as manly as they came. His waist was narrow, and that pale hair tapered into a line that went straight to his groin. His legs were strong and powerful, but it was what hung between them that had me drooling.

That had been inside me? I knew he was big, my pussy ached and throbbed from his rough use, but that? Wow. It was practically a baby arm that jutted from a thatch of hair a few shades darker than on his head. Thick and long, his dick started to swell and grow from my observation. I flicked my gaze to his, and he was watching me. Grinning. He just stood there, lacking any amount of modesty, and let me take him in. He was naked as the day he was born except for his signature cowboy hat on his head. The crown of his dick was flared, a reddish tone that from even ten feet away, had pre-cum oozing from the narrow slit.

And for some reason, he was into me. So into me his dick now curved up toward his belly. Below, his balls were large and pendulous, showing off his virility. He'd come not twenty minutes before, but they looked heavy and full as if he had more for me.

I licked my lips and had to turn away because I'd drop to my knees before him and take him into my mouth. No. Swim first, suck later. I took off my glasses and dropped them on top of my clothes.

Perhaps he was in agreement, for we both ran into the water—Boyd with his hat still on—and I gasped as I suddenly lost my footing on the smooth bottom. Concern flitted over Boyd's face until I laughed.

"It's deep!" I was up to my shoulders, and I moved my arms over the surface making little waves.

He was at my side in a flash, lifting me into a floating baby cradle, turning me around. I loved the feel of his arms around me, his chest hair tickling my back. "It is. Perfect for diving off that ledge." He lifted his chin toward the top of the waterfall.

I shook my head. It wasn't more than fifteen feet, but I was chicken. "No way I'm doing that."

"Nah, I wouldn't let you. Not unless I was underneath to make sure you weren't scared." He grinned at me.

And suddenly, I felt like nothing would scare me again. Not with Boyd around to protect me. He'd done so with Jett at the bar and said he would now here, with my inner fear of heights.

I'd been in control for so long. There'd been no one looking out for me, not even when I was a kid. I was used to taking care of myself, but here, suddenly, was this guy who had followed me home and wanted me to get my rest and held me in the pool, so I could stretch out and float like a baby in the womb.

Again, it was too good to be true.

But I wanted to trust in it. I wanted this. I wanted what he seemed to be offering. Was I a fool to think, even though he'd been saying the words, really wanted it too?

Just for today, I would. How could I ruin this place, with this guy, by thinking the worst?

I could put the brakes on tomorrow. Take a step back. Right now, I just wanted to be present with Boyd, savor how he held me, what he did to me with his hands, mouth and dick. "I love this," I murmured. "Maybe I do believe in fate."

I swore Boyd stopped breathing for a moment. Then he carried me straight out of the water like a man with a purpose.

"What are you doing?" I laughed. "That was so nice."

"I need to be inside you again," he rumbled, his voice raw. I saw bald need on his face. Hunger. The same look he had as he stalked toward me at the truck. It had been aggressive, heady. Potent. He'd spanked my ass, been rough. Wild, even. This though, it was just as intense, but it was as if he craved me, as if I were an addiction, and he needed another fix. "That okay with you?"

I could totally relate. He'd just taken me less than an hour earlier, and I wanted to do it again. "God, yes." I'd never felt so desirable in my life. He couldn't fake passion like that. Could he? No, he definitely couldn't. A dick hard like his couldn't be faked. This guy was seriously into me. And I was going to drink up every delicious second of it.

19

Boyd

I carried her to the pile of blankets I'd spread on the ground as Audrey had looked around. My original plan had been to spread these blankets out, treat her to a picnic, get to know her some more. Then, I'd fuck her. But that already happened at the truck. Both parts, the getting-to-know-you and the fucking.

Now the blankets were for the reprise. This time wasn't going to be slow and sensual either. I'd skip the toy this time. It wasn't needed.

My wolf was desperate to claim her because her ass was still pink from my spanking, and it was as close to a mark as I was going to get. Thank fuck, the moon wasn't full, or I'd try to give her a mating bite. As it was, I was having a hard time holding back.

But I didn't want to.

Audrey just told me she might believe in fate. For once

in my life, things were falling into place. They felt right. As if I might have the woman of my dreams by my side. Wanting babies and a home as much as me. I'd been gone over a decade, and it seemed what I was looking for had been at home all along. I felt like Dorothy in *The Wizard of Oz*.

There really was no place like home. It might be Wolf Ranch, but it was going to be wherever Audrey was.

God, I didn't even realize how lost I'd been all these years. Maybe since my parents' death. I'd been playing the black sheep because I thought I was one, instead of taking responsibility, standing by my pack, being a real man. Instead, I'd played at being the champ, but it had all been fake. I'd been hiding the real me. No, I'd just been fucking hiding.

But Audrey—sweet Audrey—made me want to stop running. To stand still. To stand beside her. To be the one she turned to, to lean on, to love. I wanted to be her man. Her mate. The guy who had the honor of... fucking her hard.

Yeah, other things, too, but that's all I could think of at the moment. I laid her on her back on the soft pile of blankets and searched for another condom in the pocket of my discarded shirt.

The damn bandage I wore to hide my lack of a wound peeled up on one corner, and I hurriedly pressed it back down. I'd come clean with her soon. I had to. But right now —fuck!

I looked down at her, her hair almost black dripping and spread out across the blanket. Her skin was pale and damp. I licked up a drop from her shoulder, breathed in her scent combined with nature. Lower, her nipples had crinkled into hard tips from the cooler air. I licked one, then the other. Lower, her belly was slightly curved, her hips wide and full.

Her pussy was a dark pink and swollen from our earlier fucking. Her legs were slightly parted, knees bent. Every inch of her was perfect.

"Can you see me without your glasses?" I wondered. Every time I saw her, she had them on.

"This close I can," she replied.

God, I needed her.

Desperately.

I climbed over her, nudging her knees wide, so I could settle in between and claimed her mouth. Roughly. Passionately. I nipped her lower lip and sucked her tongue. I bit down her neck. One of my hands cupped and squeezed her breast, then I shifted to pinch her nipple. She gasped, and I made note of how she liked a little bite of pain. Maybe not a masochist, but she got hot having her ass spanked. It made me wonder if she'd like a little bite... perhaps at the crook of her neck.

She'd opened her thighs wider, letting me settle so my dick slid over her slick folds. Her pussy was wet again and not just from the water. I smelled her nectar, sweet and alluring. This time, she carried the tang of fucking on her from earlier. I'd filled a condom with my cum, but still, she smelled like me. Not enough, but it was a start. She reached for me and knocked my cowboy hat off.

"Oh, now you're in trouble, darlin'." I pinned her wrists down beside her head. Her broad smile as she struggled told me that she loved it. I felt her fight against the hold, then relent.

Yeah, she submitted so beautifully. At the truck with her ass upturned, red with my handprints and a plug parting her lush ass cheeks, and now. "You don't touch a cowboy's hat."

"Oh yeah?" she dared, her voice taunting, but a soft smile turned up the corner of her lips.

"That's right. Now there's going to be punishment."

She rocked her hips up against mine. "Mmm."

"Mmm, indeed." I lowered my head to flick my tongue over her nipple, tracing it with the tip, then sucking, then nipping. When I pulled back, I slapped it lightly.

"Oh." Her eyes and mouth rounded at the same time.

It was so fucking adorable.

"That's right, darlin'. Ever had your breasts spanked?"

She rocked beneath me some more, trying to rub her sweet little clit over my hardened shaft. I thrust into the notch of her legs, my rigid cock gliding between her wet thighs. I could just slide right on in, take her bare.

"Oh fuck," I groaned. The sensation was different than being inside her, but just as fucking erotic.

"What?"

"This is so hot."

"Um, Mr. Cowboy? You're not in me yet."

I gave a pained chuckle, because my balls ached so bad, I couldn't see straight. I switched my grip to pin both her wrists over her head with one hand then pinched her nipple again. I laved it with my tongue, drew back and slapped the side again.

"What's with you and spanking?" she asked.

"What's with you and loving to be spanked?" I countered.

Her hips bucked wildly beneath mine. Yeah, my girl liked it a little rough.

"You keep doing that, and I'm gonna come before I ever get inside you," I groaned.

She sucked her lower lip into her mouth for a long pull, then released it. "You'd better get inside me then, champ."

"You're not ready yet."

She frowned, rolled her hips. "I'm ready. You got me ready down at the truck."

"You've got a tight little pussy, and I'm big. You might be all soft and swollen from the earlier fucking, but I won't hurt you."

She whimpered as I kept licking and sucking, spanking and nipping at her tits. They weren't huge, but they were real, so fucking soft and plump beneath my hands, and her nipples seemed to be hardwired right to her swollen and eager clit.

Fuck. I wanted to make her come before I did because I knew I was going to go off like a rocket the second I sank into her. My vision was sharpening, which told me my eyes might be showing the color of my wolf.

I squeezed them closed, so she wouldn't see. Released her wrists. "Now you keep those hands right there, you hear? Don't move them or you'll be punished." I crawled lower.

"Punished?"

I gave her my most roguish grin. "Or I'll spank that ass again, darlin'. Fate knows I love seeing my prints on your creamy skin."

I settled between her legs and pushed her knees wide, then licked into her. Her sweet flavor burst on my tongue. Her sensitive tissues were swollen and flush with blood from my dick giving her a workout. Her clit was hard and prominent, as if it were eager for my tongue. She immediately reached for my head, her fingers tangling in my hair, pulling my face against her warm flesh. I lifted my head and grinned up her naked body. "Uh uh. Bad girl. Looks like you're getting spanked."

I flipped her over and lifted her hips, positioning her on

her hands and knees. She looked over her shoulder at me, her damp hair sticking to her forehead and cheeks. Out here in nature, naked, fuck… my dick dripped pre-cum. My wolf was panting, eager for her. Just like this.

Her ass was still pink from earlier, reminding me how delicate her skin was. Not that I didn't have plenty of practice with human women. I gave her a few more light slaps, then pushed her cheeks wide and rimmed her ass with my tongue.

"Boyd!" she screamed, the sound echoing off the rocks.

I did it again, and she made a warbling sound—somewhere between shock and pleasure. "Next time you disobey, I'm gonna fuck that ass, darlin'," I said, although I didn't mean it. Not unless she wanted me to, of course.

"Boyd," she whimpered again, like she was getting as desperate as I was. Her hips shifted, as if she were wiggling an imaginary tail.

Fuck it.

I ripped open the condom and rolled it on. So much for sweet sex on soft blankets.

She was getting it raw and rough because it seemed holding back with her was not an option. And she didn't want it that way. My straight-laced doc was a wild one.

I lined my cock up with her entrance and dragged my sheathed head through her plump folds. Pure fucking heaven. I drew in a steadying breath before I sank into her heat. Tight. Wet. Perfect.

I was lost in her. In the feel of her. In connecting with her like this. Seeking pleasure from her body and giving her pleasure in return. I gripped her hips and pushed in, forcing myself to go slow, not to hurt her. I was big, and she did have a tight little pussy.

But she made the sweetest sounds—like uhn uhns that

made me want to fuck her so hard she saw stars. My grip tightened. My thrusts increased in speed.

"Harder."

Oh sweet fate, she felt so. Damn. Good.

My eyes rolled back in my head as I took her faster. Deeper. Our flesh slapped together as I bottomed out. Her fingers gripped the blanket, as if that would keep her anchored.

My teeth—oh shit!—my canines descended, like my wolf wanted to mark her here and now. I was fucking her outside. She was on her hands and knees, and I was pounding her from behind. Her sounds were almost words of love for my wolf. This was a claiming, all I had to do was sink my teeth into her neck and come in her.

No. I tried to force the urge back down. Meanwhile, my hips jackhammered harder and faster, plowing into her roughly. I would never get enough of this, of her.

A growl rose up in my chest. I trapped it in my throat, holding my breath. She whimpered, then moaned as she came, her inner walls clenching rhythmically, trying to pull the cum from my balls. It worked.

I let out a shout and plowed deep into her, shooting my load. Before I finished, I managed to reach around and rub her clit, assuring she got off again. I needed to hear her cry my name. To know I was the one, the only one to satisfy the deepest, darkest fantasies.

"Boyd!" she cried. Fuck, yes.

Her knees slid out from under her as her channel squeezed my cock. I caught her waist to hold her up, holding those hips snugly against mine and rubbing her clit the entire time she came.

And then I pulled us both to our sides, my cock still buried deep, my face in her beautiful dark hair. I breathed in her scent, listening to the sound of our combined breaths. Of her heartbeat.

Of the birds singing their sunset song.

I love you.

I wanted to say it out loud. Three words I'd *never* uttered to a female before. Never felt for one. But I didn't want to scare her off. And my female was definitely still skittish. It had only been a few days, and she'd called me on what I'd been and doubted I'd walk away from it all just for her. But she had to know now, after what we'd just shared, here and at the truck, that this was special. More. Everything.

Soon, I'd tell her. And I'd come clean about what I was, too. Just as soon as I thought she could handle it.

20

Audrey

We dressed slowly. I didn't think either of us wanted to leave. It had been such a wonderful afternoon. We laid on the blankets until the sun dipped behind the mountains and the sky changed from pink to purple and finally grew dusk.

The sound of the waterfall blotted out the rest of the world. Made it feel like we were in our own special little paradise, where nothing could intrude. Boyd was right—it was one of nature's most beautiful secrets.

That was why it seemed only fitting, rather than shocking, when I spotted a grey wolf slinking along the rocks at the top of the waterfall. I gasped, first with surprise, then a little panic, then pleasure at the magnificent sight. "Look!" I pointed to the ridge.

"Oh, shit," Boyd muttered.

If his response seemed strange, I didn't have time to register it because at that moment, a shot rang out from the distance, behind us. I startled and slapped my hands instinctively over my ears.

"Hold your fire!" Boyd roared, flying to his feet at the same moment I screamed, and the wolf gave a terrible yelp.

I'd never forget the sound of it. I watched as the poor creature blasted sideways, the bullet striking its hindquarters. It lost its footing in slick moss and water.

"No!" I screamed as the wolf fell over the edge, legs scrambling in the air as it took the drop into the pool. It hit the surface with a huge splash.

Everything happened so fast.

Boyd ran to the edge and dived into the pool after the wolf, which was insane.

"Stop! Boyd!"

Shit! It was one thing to admire its magnificence from afar, another to go after it. Did he not understand it was a wild animal he was attempting to rescue? The creature was badly injured. If it was alive, it would surely tear his throat out when he tried to help it.

I stood at the water's edge, holding my breath, trying to see beyond the bubbling surface of the pool. Time lengthened. Stretched. It felt like forever but was probably only a moment before Boyd popped from beneath the surface and walked out of the pool holding a lifeless wolf.

"Oh my God, Boyd!"

He dropped the bloody animal on the blankets and instantly started chest compressions. "Shift, kid. *Now.*"

"Boyd, be careful," I warned. "That's a wolf, for God's sake. He'll wake up and bite you." I wanted to help and was obviously trained in CPR, but I wasn't a veterinarian. This was way out of my wheelhouse.

The wolf jerked several times, water pouring out of its mouth.

"Shift," Boyd commanded again, his voice louder.

And then bones cracked and crunched and the wolf changed. *Into a human!*

I stared. Blinked. Yes, I had my glasses on. A naked male. Dark hair, slim build, late teens. Not a wolf.

"Audrey, take over," Boyd ordered, straightening. Water dripped off him, his clothes clung to him. He was breathing hard, his gaze dark. Fierce. I'd never seen him like this before. His fingers were on the guy's neck.

"What?"

"You're a doctor, and he's been shot. He's got a pulse, but he's not breathing. Help him."

"But... but—"

"Now," he commanded.

I blinked again and pulled myself together. I slid seamlessly into his place, dropping to my knees on the wet ground to provide rescue breaths. Human bodies I could handle—regardless of how they appeared in front of me. *Had he just been a wolf?* My training made it easy to go on autopilot, doing everything I could to save his life.

Boyd was already jogging away and up the steep bank along the side of the waterfall. "I gotta keep Markle from seeing him. *Do not call 911.* And don't worry about the gunshot wound, just get his lungs cleared."

I knelt beside the blankets where just a short time ago we were naked and... making love. No, that hadn't been making love, it had been fucking. But it had been more than that.

Now I was trying to resuscitate a kid who'd been a wolf. I heard Boyd speak, but it took a while for his words to filter in.

Markle.

Jett Markle had shot the boy—wolf. Whatever he was. Whatever the fuck just happened.

I heard Boyd's voice shout in the distance. "You just shot my motherfucking dog, Markle!"

The sound of the two of them shouting continued, but I missed the rest because the boy at last coughed, and his lungs started to clear. I rolled him to his side and let him work the rest of the water out with gasps and coughs.

"That's it," I encouraged. "You're going to be okay."

Was that true? The kid just got shot. But Boyd had said not to worry about that part. And then the pieces started to fall into place. It was as if my brain finally understood what had been in front of me all this time. I wasn't crazy.

I now knew why Boyd's wound that miraculously healed. Why he didn't want me to examine it. How he'd walked out of the hospital right after being gored by a bull. The way he'd known this wolf was actually a man. No, boy. I looked at him more closely and guessed him to be sixteen or so. Not much more.

Had Boyd ordered him to change form?

Shift, kid.

Yes. Boyd had known what he was. Known what to do to help him. Knew because he'd done it himself.

That meant... Boyd was one of them. Boyd Wolf wasn't just a cowboy, a rodeo champ. Wolf wasn't just his last name. He was a *werewolf*. Or whatever I was looking at right now.

It seemed far less strange than it should, but I was sure that was because I was in crisis mode. There was no time to get dramatic. I had a patient to save. Despite Boyd's instructions, I couldn't let the bullet wound go untended. Breathing had been his first priority, but now that his lungs were clear, I grabbed one corner of the blanket and yanked it up to ball over the wound, providing compression, rolling him to his back to look for an exit wound. There wasn't one. Which meant the bullet was still inside.

I needed to get him to a hospital.

The young man reached down. I thought he was going to feel for his wound, but instead he tried to tug more of the blanket around his waist. Oh right. Because he was, well, naked. It seemed wolves couldn't very well run around wearing clothing.

Boyd stalked back, anger radiating from him, I presumed from his interaction with Jett Markle, who he must've managed to send away. His clothes still dripped water as he crouched beside the kid and took his jaw in his big hand. He wasn't gentle. "Who the fuck are you?"

"Boyd, I need to get him to a hospital," I said.

"You don't, Audrey." He gentled his voice with me, which seemed sweet, considering the circumstances. "If he's breathing, he's going to be fine."

"He's been shot." I knew I was stating the obvious, but the obvious was well... strange as hell.

"And I was gored by a bull. He'll be fine," he told me. Then, to the boy, "Who are you?"

The young man coughed a few more times, not opening his eyes. "James. James Clifton."

"You care to explain why you were running in wolf form across my neighbor's ranch?"

"Visiting—" He coughed again. "—my girlfriend."

Boyd groaned. "You just endangered the whole fucking pack, my friend. Just so you could get laid."

His eyes blinked open, and he tried to sit up, but Boyd pushed him back down. "Please—don't tell my parents. You can call my sister instead. Karen. She'll pick me up."

Glancing at Boyd, I cocked an eyebrow, silently asking

"who?" He must have caught on because he said, "The woman from the bar."

Ah, Total Bitch was a wolf? Seriously?

Boyd stilled and stared at the kid. "Don't tell your parents? I'm going to tell someone worse than that. Your alpha."

The boy groaned, and I looked him over to see what the problem was but realized he wasn't happy about Boyd's words.

"He's gonna make the decision about how this gets handled. End of story. How are you feeling now?"

The youth had lost blood, and his face was pale, but he pushed himself up to lean on one elbow. This time, Boyd didn't stop him. "Better."

"Lemme see," Boyd said to me, putting his hand over mine where I held compression on the gunshot.

He wasn't a doctor, but I guessed he knew more about this young man's physiology than I did, so I let him lift away the pressure.

He pushed and prodded the wound, making the kid flinch, then shook his head. Most of the blood had washed off in the water, but the area was red and angry. "Bullet must be in the bone, but it'll come out on its own." Boyd turned his head to look at me. "He doesn't need care. I swear to fate, Doctor."

I swear to fate.

Interesting turn of phrase.

He'd mentioned fate when he talked about meeting me. Was the belief part of his culture? *Wolf* culture?

He reached out, lightly wrapped a hand around my elbow and squeezed. "You okay? I imagine this is a shock."

"Uh, yeah. Yeah, it is." I looked at him through new eyes.

My sexy rodeo champ was actually a wolf. Boyd *Wolf.* "You must think me stupid." I looked away.

He turned my chin back with his fingers. "You're the smartest person I know."

"Were you going to tell me?"

He looked slightly guilty. "Yes. I wanted to. From the very beginning. It's just... forbidden. I was trying to figure out what to do."

"I won't tell your secret." I looked him straight in the eye, then at James, so they both knew they were safe with me. "Doctor-patient confidentiality. I won't breathe a word. You both have my promise. Besides, who'd believe me?"

"Thank you. That means a lot." Boyd squeezed my elbow again. "I'll tell you anything you want to know. Answer all the questions. But let's get James out of here before anyone else sees him. You have to work tomorrow?"

I nodded. "Office hours."

He looked down at the boy, a teen, who'd just wanted to sneak away for time with his girlfriend. It sounded so very familiar. Hadn't it been exactly what Boyd and I had done?

"How are you doing, kid? Can you walk yet?"

James nodded and climbed up, wrapping the blanket around his waist. Boyd was right. He seemed to be improving by the minute. His color was already returning. My medical mind reeled from what I'd just witnessed. He'd been shot, as a wolf, fell off the side of a cliff, almost drowned and was now standing. Impossible. But it was right in front of me.

Boyd helped me to stand. "Go and get in my truck," he ordered James. "Follow the path, and you'll see it. Try to run off, and I'll hunt your ass down."

After the young man started away, his shoulders slumped in defeat. Boyd slid an arm around my waist and pulled me against his wet body. He brushed back my hair and pushed my glasses up my nose for me. "You sure you're okay? Not freaked out?"

"Definitely freaked. Um, it's a lot to process. I... I guess I like it," I admitted, which sounded dumb. But it seemed like the missing piece to understanding Boyd just fell into place. He was too perfect before. Too good looking. Too strong. Too charming. I felt I couldn't trust him, like something wasn't real. Now it made sense why he was such a spectacular specimen of a male. How he could ride bulls for so many years without breaking his neck. How he could walk away from such a terrible goring. It made it easier to believe what he said, even about his interest in me. About how he knew from the first that I was the one.

He wasn't just looking at me as a man, but as a wolf, too.

I pushed up his wet shirt and ripped off the bandage covering the place he was gored by the bull. *Nothing!* Not even a mark. I traced my fingertip over it, in awe. Boyd Wolf was something special. And I felt honored to know his secret.

Boyd's face broke into a smile. "Yeah? You like it?"

I nodded. "I have a lot of questions. *A lot.* But I want to see your wolf."

Boyd cupped the side of my face with one hand and traced my lips with his thumb. "I'll show you, darlin'. Any time you want. And I'll answer all your questions later. I promise."

I tipped my head toward the truck. "How soon will he heal fully?"

"Oh, shortly. A teen in perfect health? It'll just be a mark tomorrow. And then nothing by the next day. His pride's probably hurt worse. Come on, I'd better get him to Rob."

I frowned. "Rob, your brother?"

"Yep. As you can guess, he's a wolf, too. All of us at the ranch. Rob, he's the pack alpha. My dad before him. James is going to have to answer to him for this."

I had a lot to take in. And I wanted to know all of it. I was thrilled by it all. Definitely excited. And titillated. Awed. Confused. Intrigued.

We walked back to the truck in silence, then climbed into the front seat. James was in the back—the truck was a huge four door behemoth. I couldn't help checking in with my patient again, even though I knew he had to be fine if he walked all the way from the waterfall. Boyd had been worried about him when he'd been unconscious, but his concern slipped away once I cleared his lungs. I had to believe Boyd wouldn't be so relaxed if James' life was still in danger. "You feeling okay? Any dizziness, nausea, anything else I should know about?"

"He's fine," Boyd assured me. "James, this is Dr. Ames. You be respectful with her or you'll have even more to answer for."

The young man nodded in awkward agreement. "It hurts, ma'am, but I'll be okay."

Boyd nodded, clearly satisfied with the answer, started the truck and pulled out. It seemed that teen boys were stupid over girls, wolf or human.

"Did you actually tell Jett Markle he shot your *dog*?" I asked, laughter bubbling up now that the major crisis was past.

"I did," Boyd chuckled. "And then I took his shotgun and bent the barrel, so it's unusable. What an asshole. I mean, aside from shooting a wolf, which of course, I take *very* personally, he'd have ridden his horse by my truck to get above the waterfall, meaning he knew there were people around. And he still fired? I seriously should've shoved that shotgun up his ass instead of just giving him a black eye."

He bent the barrel of a shotgun?

"I thought no one lived on that property right now," James spoke up from the back seat. "I mean, Shefield died, right?"

"That's no excuse for you running around in wolf form in broad daylight," Boyd said sternly. "But yes, Shefield died. I don't know, Markle says he's buying it, so maybe he thinks it's already his, but I'll be damned if I'd let that happen. I gotta figure out if he's full of shit or not, and what I can do to stop it."

"You're staying then," I commented.

He turned to look at me, as if he didn't need to stare at the road to drive.

"Those words mean you're staying, that you're not picking up and heading off to the next competition."

He nodded, then looked away. "I hadn't said it aloud, that I was retiring. That this was where I now belonged. I told you I wanted a reason to stay. That it was you. You're mine, Audrey Ames. I've told you that from the start. As for being a wolf, as for being a member of the pack, I have a purpose here. If it's to finish Jett Markle, then so be it."

I stole a glance at Boyd's profile. His jaw was set with new determination. He appeared far more serious than usual, although our conversation was pretty hefty. While I missed the boyish grin, I also admired this Boyd. He wasn't just a playboy. He was a leader. He handled crisis situations with confidence and ease. Better than some doctors I'd been in surgery with.

Boyd pulled up in the circle drive in front of the ranch house. The memories of my first trip here, how he'd seduced me in his barn in about five minutes flat came flooding back but mingled with so much more pleasure now. I was sore between my legs, a constant reminder of what we'd done. Of how he'd ensured I would never forget he'd pretty much ruined me for anyone else.

Because now I knew what he was. We shared a secret. Trust. This wasn't a quickie. It wasn't just sex.

"Audrey, stay in the truck, darlin'. I'm just gonna deliver James to Rob, and then I'll drive you home. I want to stay with you." He looked at me with a gaze so fierce it made me hold my breath. "But if I do, I won't let you sleep, and you need your rest."

"I need to up my vitamins if I'm to keep up with you... and your wolf."

21

Boyd

A lot of shit went down, and I knew Rob was going to blow a gasket. My brother was grouchy at best. With what I suspected was moon madness starting to plague him, he was even less patient with people, specifically me.

I hadn't exactly caught him up to speed on the Audrey situation, so that was going to add fuel to the fire. I didn't want to leave her side, not just in the truck while she waited but tonight. Her work was important. She helped people. Saved lives. Brought babies into the world. I couldn't be totally selfish and fuck her all night long, no matter how much I wanted to. But I sure as fuck would be waiting for her after her office closed tomorrow.

James shuffled down the drive beside me with the blanket around his waist. I could offer him a pair of jeans, but I let him suffer a little. He definitely deserved it. Dumb teens and their hormones. Although, I knew just how he was feeling.

I put my fingers between my teeth and whistled loudly. Yeah, we used cell phones and all, but some old-fashioned methods still worked just as well on a ranch. If Rob heard my signal, he'd come out to find out what was going on. He did, not a minute later.

Rob stalked out of the house, characteristic annoyance in his expression. He set his hat on his head as he took the steps down from the porch. When he got an eyeful of James in nothing but a blanket, then Audrey sitting in the passenger seat of my truck, he scowled even deeper. Crossed his arms over his broad chest.

"You wanna tell me what the fuck is going on?"

Because I could be as dickish as my brother, I nudged James. He also had to own up to his shit. "You tell him what happened."

The teen swallowed, his gaze not reaching Rob's face. "I was out runnin'," he said.

"Elaborate," Rob ordered.

"I was visiting my girlfriend, so I ran down the mountain in wolf form because, well... we were sneaking out together. I cut through Shefield's property on my way home. Jett Markle shot me."

"*What?*" Rob roared, turning his furious gaze to me.

I nodded my confirmation. "He fell into Shefield's swimming hole. Audrey had to resuscitate him."

Rob's eyes narrowed. His neck grew red, and his fingers clenched into fists. "What about Markle?" he gritted, clearly not concerned about a gunshot wound.

"He saw the shot hit its mark, then the fall from the top. Nothing else," I answered. "As Audrey tended to James, I found Markle and read him the riot act. Told him he shot my dog, and he'd better keep away from me and our property, or I'd shove that gun up his nose and fire."

"What were you doing at the pool?"

"I was with Audrey, doing what you asked." I threw that in his face, since he did tell me to stick close to her. What I needed to do was come clean with Rob about my relationship with her. That I wanted to mate her and make her mine. That I'd had the urge to mark her.

He'd have to listen to that. Our wolf urges didn't lie, and they didn't lead us wrong. Even if it was against pack rules.

I would tell him later, but not in front of the kid.

Rob took a deep breath, and I knew he could smell her on me. Knew exactly what we'd been doing.

"So she saw," he said grimly.

I nodded. "She saw, and our secret is safe with her. Doctor-patient confidentiality."

"That's going to keep her from talking? This isn't a mental health visit to a clinic. She just found out we're shifters."

James bobbed his head in agreement. "She promised us, Alpha."

Rob shook his head and stared through the windshield at Audrey, who looked back at him with round eyes. I wanted to tell him to fuck off because she was clearly wary, even scared of him. I didn't like anyone fucking with my mate, even the alpha.

But because he *was* the alpha, I stayed silent. I'd ensure she was okay once I got back to the truck.

He lowered his voice even though she was human and wouldn't hear. "I know I told you to stay on her after the bull riding accident to make sure she didn't know what you were, but I *did not mean* fuck her until she falls for you. What happens when you move on to your next conquest? You think she'll still keep our secret then? No. This is a problem, Boyd. And so is Jett Markle." He turned to James, "You are in some serious shit with me, James."

The teen dropped his head to the side to bare his throat and signal submission. "Yes, Alpha. But please, could you call my sister, Karen, instead of my parents? They will outright kill me."

Rob frowned, then he pulled out his phone and handed it to James. "You call her. I'll need a sit-down with both of you about this." He turned to me. "Get Audrey home."

It was all I could do not to growl back at Rob. I wasn't going to fucking move onto another conquest, and his saying that pissed me off. But then he always thought I was the fuck-up, didn't he?

Because I was.

Even after baring my secrets to Audrey, the truth remained. I'd been the reason our parents died. Now I was part of the reason the pack was at risk. It might have been James prowling after his girlfriend that Markle had seen, but now the bastard had a hard-on for me. I'd taken his girl at the bar the other night. I'd punched him in the face after he supposedly killed my dog. I was getting in his way every chance I got, and that made things worse with him, not better.

Rob would have done the exact same thing, protected a woman from an asshole and saved one of our pack members. But pointing that out wouldn't change anything.

Fucking hell.

I stalked to the truck without a word, not trusting myself not to be disrespectful with him, which would be particularly bad in front of a young pack member.

Audrey jumped when I slammed the door too hard, and I automatically reached for her hand. "Sorry. Fuck!"

"Is he mad that I know?" Audrey asked. She was so fucking smart.

I wanted to roll my eyes, to growl, but I didn't. Her scent, the way her hair was all tangled and wild from our swim, then fucking, eased my frustrations. Just being with her, cocooned in the cab of my truck together, made me feel better. My wolf settled. "Yeah, but I can deal with it."

"What will you do?" She stared at me with those pale eyes, then pushed her glasses up.

The memories of the car crash kept flooding my mind. The crush of the metal car all around, forcing me to the floorboards. The silence from the front seat. How I'd worked my fingers bloody trying to get out, then I'd painfully shifted for the first time and been able to paw my way through the smashed window. With four animal legs, I'd been easily able to work my way up the embankment, but I'd had no idea how to shift back. I'd waited there, staring at the crushed truck for what felt like hours before someone drove by and called the fire department for help. They had to use the jaws of life to cut them out, and they'd been dead.

Fuck! Why am I remembering all this now?

Because the feeling was the same. The shame. Not feeling worthy of standing beside my golden boy brothers.

"Boyd?" Audrey prompted.

Fuck. Had she asked me a question? Right. What was I going to do?

Because I couldn't think, because my brain was too fuzzy at the moment and the weight on my chest too heavy, I said, "I don't know. This isn't on you, darlin'."

Later, I would wish I'd said a million other things. Explained that she was my mate, and I would fight to keep her no matter what. Even if it meant being at odds with my family and my pack.

But I was out of steam in the moment. I'd defaulted to fuck-up mode.

I just needed to get my head on straight and get things figured out.

I pulled up in front of Audrey's place and climbed out, walking around to open the door for her.

"You okay?" She took my offered hand and peered up at me as I walked her to the door. My sweet doctor was concerned about me. "You sure you don't want to stay?" she asked.

I sucked in a breath as my dick punched against my jeans. "Fuck, do I." I forced a smile. "You need to sleep, and I need to deal with things at the ranch. I'll call you, okay?"

"Um, yeah. Okay." She kept her gaze on my face, a wrinkle of worry between her brows. I bent over and gave her a quick kiss.

"Good night, darlin'. I'll talk to you tomorrow."

She nodded, her smile wistful as she backed through her front door. "All right, sounds good."

Before she shut the door, I said, "Gotta let that pretty pussy rest. I've got plans for it tomorrow."

She bit her lip, and her gaze dropped to my crotch. "Good night," she whispered.

Fuck me.

I got in my truck, even though my wolf was practically snarling at me to stay, to sleep with her. Hold her all night. I couldn't. I had things to figure out. Instead of heading straight home to deal with shit, I found myself driving up to the mountains, to a pullout where I liked to go when I needed to run. I stripped out of my clothes and shifted, bolting through the evergreens.

Praying my wolf would help me cast off the fog of uncertainty that had settled over me and Audrey and the future I'd been planning with her.

22

Audrey

I STEPPED out of my house and locked the door. I hadn't been able to sleep much last night, reliving everything that had happened on our date. The wild sex at his truck, the waterfall, the wolf, then finding out it was a kid. That Boyd was also a wolf. I'd seen the kid shift from a wolf into human form. I'd seen Boyd's bull riding injury, then saw it gone, as if it had never happened. It was unexplainable, yet it made sense.

I wasn't freaked. I should be. A boyfriend who was a part wolf? Insane.

But it felt real. It felt... right.

I'd tossed and turned mostly because I worried about Boyd. I didn't know what exactly passed between him and his brother, but I did know it was about me. I saw Rob staring through the windshield at me, frowning and laying down the law about something to Boyd and James. It was obvious he was the pack's alpha. It made complete sense why he was such a hardass. He was the leader of a group who had to remain secret. One slip-up, and they could be destroyed or killed.

It was forbidden for Boyd to tell me. I understood that.

Was it also forbidden for him to be with me? Was that why he seemed so out of sorts when he came back to the truck? Why he hadn't spent the night with me?

"Hi, Dr. Ames?"

I jumped in surprise. I'd been so deep in my thoughts, I hadn't noticed the woman leaning against my car at the curb.

Oh shit. It was Total Bitch from the bar. Karen. James' sister.

She wore snug jeans, cowgirl boots and a plain white t-shirt. The neckline was a deep V that accentuated her ample breasts. She was beautiful, I had to give her that. She was also a bitch, so I approached her warily.

"Hi. I just wanted to thank you for saving my brother's life yesterday. He told me he almost drowned."

And got shot, but apparently that wasn't life-threatening to a wolf.

"Oh, no problem. That's what I do." I smiled wanly. "I am a doctor."

She showed no intention of moving her ass off my car. "Yeah, I heard that."

Okay, what the hell does Total Bitch want? It clearly wasn't to thank me. Most family members who were thankful brought me a Bundt cake or sent pictures of their baby.

"Listen, I don't know if Boyd told you, but—" She rolled her lips in like she was breaking bad news to me. She looked left and right, as if my neighbors were leaning out their windows to overhear us. "—shifters can't mate with humans."

I frowned. "Like, it's not biologically possible? Because I can say you're wrong." I could play a little bitchy, too.

Her eyes narrowed because she caught my meaning. James probably mentioned the waterfall, and it was easy to put two and two together about what we'd been doing there. It hadn't been Bible study.

"Like, it's forbidden," she clarified. "I hate to tell you this, but since you were so kind to James and all, I thought you deserved to know. I feel like it would be even worse if you found out later."

My stomach tightened, and I didn't want to ask. But I did. "What?"

She tucked her dark hair back behind her ear. "Rob sent Boyd to date you. To keep you quiet about his bull riding accident because while it was probably pretty bad when it first happened, he healed way too fast to be human. You couldn't know the truth. Boyd's always been the charming one of the three Wolf brothers." She shrugged her slim shoulders. "I guess Rob figured a little attention from the good-looking one, and you'd be smitten enough to do whatever he asked."

She looked me over, head to toe. "A little attention goes a long way with some women."

Oh God. I wanted to puke. She was manipulating me and being a total bitch. She knew a woman's weaknesses and went right for them. I was smart enough to see that. She'd been all over Boyd at the bar before I got there. Hell, even after. Then her little stunt with the mechanical bull. Boyd had rebuffed her efforts, and she was scorned. He'd wanted me, not her.

The cattiness was one thing, but something in her words rang true.

Boyd had used sex to distract me from examining his wounds. He'd gotten me in the barn, got my panties down around my thighs and made me forget my own name, let alone to look at his wound. Or lack of. He'd even covered the spot with a bandage to fake me out. It was only because of her brother's eagerness to fool around with his girlfriend and a meddling Jett Markle that the truth had come out. Boyd hadn't told me he was a shifter.

Had Boyd been seducing me just to keep what they were a secret? How would Karen know that if she hadn't actually heard it from one of the brothers? She hadn't been there.

"You're not one of us. You never will be. He may have had fun with you, but he'll be back in my bed. He can mate me, bite me as we fuck. I'll give him pure pups." She stuck her chest out and practically preened with pride over her ability to birth a shifter baby.

I might deliver babies for a living, but I knew jack about shifters. Was a shifter/shifter mating required? Could there be mixed babies? Was that even possible? Was she messing with me or telling me the truth?

Boyd hadn't filled me in. He hadn't answered any of my questions. He'd promised to do so, but instead of coming in last night and staying when he could've given me the answers I needed, he'd left. Was he stalling?

I blinked. I couldn't process all this or look at Karen a second longer.

"Excuse me, I'm late," I snapped at the same moment Boyd pulled up in his giant truck. I hadn't expected to see him this morning, but my heart flipped at the sight. I had it for him bad, and I realized now that was more trouble than I ever imagined.

"Uh oh. Speak of the devil," Karen said, a sly smile curving her glossed lips. "Just be careful, that's all I'm saying. Have a fling, 'cause he's that good. But I don't want you to get your heart broken like every other human female who slept with Boyd Wolf."

"What did you just say?" Boyd growled as he climbed out of his truck and slammed the door. He couldn't have possibly heard that unless—

Oh yeah. They probably have super hearing, too. Wolf ears.

He stalked toward Karen, but she dashed away. "Gotta run! Thanks for saving James yesterday!" She jumped in a beat-up VW bug and drove off.

"What the fuck did she just say to you?" Boyd demanded as he watched her car disappear around the corner.

I drew back. I didn't like this side of him, the tense, snarling anger that seemed to simmer beneath the surface. I didn't like the way he was talking to me. I especially didn't like all the thoughts rushing through my head right now. I wanted to throat punch Karen for messing with my head.

"Is it true, Boyd?"

"No," he said immediately before I even clarified what I was asking.

"You're lying."

He shook his head, like it would make things clear. "Lying about what? What did she tell you, Audrey?"

"That Rob told you to seduce me to keep me from talking about your accident. To make me forget about looking at it or to ensure I was crazy for thinking you'd been so gravely injured."

Boyd started to speak, then his mouth snapped closed, then opened again, and my heart dropped to my shoes. Oh shit. Karen had been right.

I'd questioned myself, wondered if I needed a new prescription for my glasses. Doubted my medical assessment. All that time, he'd been telling me I'd exaggerated.

Tears filled my eyes, and I started stumbling blindly for my car door. "When you open your mouth, you better not lie to me."

"Hang on. *Hang on*, Audrey." Boyd tried to block my way, but he seemed smart enough not to touch me.

I spun, glared. "Step back, Boyd. I really don't want to see you right now."

"Just give me a minute to explain."

I shook my head. "I knew it was too good to be true. I knew a guy like you had to be pretending if he was interested in a woman like me. I was right. So was Karen."

Boyd pushed my door shut when I opened it. "That's not true," he insisted, keeping his hand on the top of the door. "I told you, Audrey. It was fate. I felt it at the arena. I knew it then. I've known it all along. You're mine."

I shook my head. "I'm not yours, Boyd. I'm not anybody's. You knew what I wanted all along, and you used it against me. I was as easy as all those buckle bunnies, wasn't I? Now step out of my way. I have to get to work."

Misery washed over Boyd's face, but after a moment, he opened my car door and stepped back.

"I don't want to see you again. And don't call me." I got in and slammed the door.

"Wait, Audrey!" he shouted, but I'd already started the car. I drove away.

I sure as hell wasn't watching in the rear-view mirror to see what he would do.

I'd been a fool, but it was over now.

Boyd Wolf was already history. I would find someone else. Someone normal and kind. Maybe dorky like me.

Someone human.

Christ, I didn't know a breakup could hurt this badly. I was so stupid. I should've just fucked him in the med room at the arena. Been one of those women who had a little ride on Boyd's huge dick, then pulled up their jeans and walked away. They'd get an orgasm from him but keep their hearts intact. I'd been so much worse than them, and I'd judged them harshly. I'd fallen for him and that made me the dumbest of them all. I pulled in at the hospital and dropped my head to the steering wheel, giving into the sobs that had choked my throat the entire drive.

23

$\mathcal{B}$OYD

FUCKING FUCK. If I'd thought I was a screwup before, it was nothing like what I felt now. Disappointing Rob was par for the course. But hurting Audrey Ames? The female I wanted to spend the rest of my life with?

That cut like a fucking knife through my chest.

I sat in my truck, my thumb hovering over the screen of my phone.

Don't call me, she'd said.

She hadn't said don't text.

ME: *I'm sorry. Let's talk.*

AFTER FIVE MINUTES, then ten, nothing. "Shit!" I shouted. It didn't make me feel any better. She wasn't going to respond.

I could show up at her office, but that wasn't the place to talk. I couldn't disrespect her like that, in front of her patients or office staff, no matter how much I wanted to explain.

Should I write her a letter? A good old-fashioned letter? I could get the words out right, get them down on paper, so she could read them again and again until she believed me.

What was required in this situation that would make everything right?

I wish I fucking knew. I couldn't fix what happened to my parents, and it seemed I couldn't fix this.

Would it help to tell her about fate? About how my wolf picked her, and he only picked one female. The way we mated for life?

Or would talking about wolf stuff just annoy the fuck out of her right now? I'd only heard the tail end of what Karen had said to her, and I could imagine the rest. She was poison to the pack, and I had to deal with her, too.

I started to type another text, then deleted it. No, a text wouldn't do because I wasn't a teenager. I couldn't fit all of what I wanted to say using my thumbs on my cell. A letter. I needed to get it all in a letter. Hell, I'd write her a thousand letters if I could just figure out what to say. And for that, I needed to go home, sit down and get my shit figured out where she was concerned.

What did I want? Me. Not the pack. Not what Rob would do or want or expect.

I slammed my fist into the dash, cracking it. Funny, it didn't feel as satisfying as I'd hoped. No, doing my usual irresponsible things felt wrong right now. Including that run I'd taken last night to avoid talking to Rob, even if that meant telling him to fuck off.

It was time to man up and solve my fucking problems.

I started the truck and drove home.

AUDREY

The universe was looking out for me because I ended up with three births and stayed at the hospital until two in the morning. I had no idea what was in the water or the weather nine months earlier, but the population of Cooper Valley had exploded the past few weeks. It was good to see young people and growing families in the community, but it was a reminder of everything I didn't have. When I got home, I found an envelope on my doormat with my name neatly scrawled across the front. I looked around, but all was dark and quiet. A dog barked in the distance, and I instantly thought of it being a wolf.

No, Boyd had put thoughts in my head... and a letter in my hands. I couldn't believe he'd written to me. Who besides your Aunt Dorothy wrote letters?

Boyd did.

Don't read it. Do *not* read it.

I tossed it in the trash can inside my door and went straight to bed. And stayed there. Fortunately, I was so tired from working... and from two previous nights of terrible sleep, that I was out cold.

The alarm jarred me awake, and I got up on auto-pilot, showered and went back to the hospital. Coffee fueled me, and I tried to keep my mind a blank. I couldn't stop to think. I couldn't slow down and realize my life had been turned upside down in a few short days. Not any hot guy, but a hot guy who ended up being a wolf. Nope, I wasn't thinking about that. Nor about the way he made me feel when he got all protective. The way he lit my body on fire. His smile. His touch. His dick as it filled me.

I couldn't think about him because when I did, it literally felt like I had a huge gaping hole in the middle of my chest, as if I'd been the one gored by the bull. I'd fallen all right, and I didn't have the ability to magically regenerate the way Boyd did.

I worked late again, volunteering to stay and cover for a fellow doctor who wanted to see her son's little league game and celebrate over pizza. Another thing I'd never get to do. When I got home, there was another letter on my doormat. I threw it away. Showered. Climbed in bed. This time, I barely slept. Went in early.

Doctors were no strangers to lack of sleep and long hours. In this case, it was a haven for me. A place I could bury my head and not ever think again.

Not ever feel again. Numb was good. Numb was safe.

24

Boyd

"You wanna tell me what the fuck is going on?" Rob asked, walking up behind me. "You've been a sulky fucker for days now."

I'd been pitching rocks at a telephone pole for the past three hours. Pitching them so hard I'd embedded hundreds of stones into the wood, so it looked like it had been turned into a mosaic. I leaned against the fence, one foot propped up on the bottom rail. My hat was tipped back, and I'd heard him walking over from the house, but I'd ignored him. I couldn't do that now, the nosy asshole.

Two days. I'd poured my heart out to Audrey in a letter. When she didn't answer that one, I'd written another. I'd keep writing them until she answered. I was trying to do the right thing, to tell her the truth, to give her everything I couldn't say aloud. Everything I wished I'd said from the beginning.

Except I suspected she hadn't even read them.

Which meant I might have to make a grander gesture. If only I knew what would win her back. Crawling, begging and groveling weren't off the table.

I'd planned on talking to Rob about Audrey, but I'd been pissed off at him. I'd been too hurt to see straight. It took everything in me not to hop in my truck and go to her. My wolf was not happy with me for staying away. Besides dropping the letters on her stoop, I'd steered clear of everyone. Especially my brother.

Even though it wasn't really his fault. Still, if he hadn't talked about her in front James, fucking Karen wouldn't have had the fuel to start a fire.

That stupid female had been trying to land a Wolf brother since we were kids. She'd been working hard at snagging me since I'd been back. I'd told her at the bar I wasn't interested, made it obvious when I left with Audrey. But no. It figured she'd step in to cause me trouble when I finally found my mate.

She was a bitch, plain and simple. To go to Audrey's house? I could only imagine the extent of the lies she'd fed to my mate. Lies that were only perpetuated by my actions. Or, hell, my lack of action.

Rob stood there waiting, his patience one of his best traits as alpha, but also really fucking annoying. He wasn't leaving this time, and that was good because I had a lot to say. A lot to unload if I was going to work through the shit in my head.

"I'm sorry I got our parents killed," I said, without looking at him. "I'm sorry you became alpha at eighteen. Sorry you didn't go to college because you had to raise me. I'm surprised you want to look at my face. There, I said it.

I'm sorry, but that's not going to bring them back. I'm not gonna play the role of the fuck-up any more."

"Excuse me?" Rob sounded shocked.

I lobbed another stone at the telephone pole. "I know you never expect much from me, but I can be just as responsible as you or Colton. I could lead the pack if I had to. I'm good for more than just seducing women to keep them quiet."

He stepped closer, set his hands on his hips. "I'm sorry, I don't know what the fuck you're talking about, but I have a feeling it has something to do with your doctor friend."

"You had me seduce Audrey to make her forget I had an injury, to make her think she'd been seeing things and not wonder how I healed in a few fucking hours. You had me do it because I was the handsome one. Then you tell me not to fuck her brains out? I can never win with you."

"Hold on. I never told you to seduce her. I told you to keep an eye on her not get your dick in her."

I growled, chucked another rock. "Fucking Karen," I mumbled.

"Whoa. What's got you so riled over the doctor?"

"She's not my doctor *friend*. She's my fucking mate. My wolf recognized her the moment I saw her in the arena. That's why I got gored—because Abe fucking Gleason asked her out and was making the moves in the stands."

Rob gave a low whistle. "Your mate? Are you sure?"

I turned, glared.

"I had no idea," he replied, sounding totally surprised. "Why the fuck didn't you say something?"

I turned on him. "Say what, exactly? It's against pack rules, right? We don't mate humans? We don't reveal what we are to them? What the fuck was I supposed to do, especially when you tell me to be her best fucking friend?"

Rob looked bewildered at seeing me express so much emotion. "Well, I don't know, but we sure as shit could've talked it over together." His tone was mild. Coaxing, almost, like I was still a kid.

I threw another rock so hard it split the wood when it hit.

"Are you going to mate her?"

"Well, besides the fact that it's not allowed, that's pretty much off the table now. Fucking Karen showed up at her house telling her you'd sent me to seduce her to keep her quiet. Thanks very much."

Rob groaned. "She is such a goddamn bitch. She needs a mate who'll get her under control, and that's not going to be any of us. Maybe it's time for her to go visit the Canadian pack for a few months. But you know that's not what I said. I wouldn't have asked it of you if I'd known how your wolf felt. I'm sorry."

I took my hat off, ran my hand over my hair. "Yeah, well. Audrey's finished with me now. She never believed in me. Just like you don't."

"Seriously, asshole? I'm about to knock you on the ground. You're the only one who doesn't believe in you."

"What the fuck are you talking about?" I snarled.

"I sent you to take care of Markle because I knew you could do it. He's an asshole and isn't going to go down easily. I didn't expect him to be resolved in one night."

"He had his eyes on Audrey, and I cleared that up pretty fast. Besides his wolf issue, I'm sure my stealing away Audrey pisses him off even more. He hates my guts."

"Good. Let him focus his anger on you. Maybe that'll distract him from Audrey, first off, and secondly, off of buying the Shefield property."

"You're not pissed about him?"

"At you?" He looked at me like I was crazy. "Hell, no. You did good. I heard you gave him a black eye."

I couldn't help but smile about that.

"That must've felt fucking good."

I nodded.

"What the fuck did you say when I walked up—about killing Mom and Dad?"

I glanced at him, then away. "It's true."

"Boyd, you cannot possibly blame yourself for their deaths." He grabbed my shoulder and pulled me around to face him. "Do you?"

My eyes smarted. "All the fucking time," I admitted. "I was late at the fair. That put us in the canyon during the storm."

"Mom called and said they would be late because they'd been chatting with another pack family that had moved away."

"She did?"

"Yeah."

"I remember them talking with the Gundersons when I finally showed up, but not her calling. It must've been when I went to take a leak."

"She told me they were waiting for you but were glad you got behind because they'd have missed their friends otherwise."

"I thought... I was unharmed in the rock slide, but I'd been trapped. I shifted, my first time, to get out of the wreckage."

"Fuck." He yanked me in for a hard hug. "None of that shit was your fault, you goddamn idiot." He held me so tightly, I couldn't breathe. After a moment, I hugged him back.

All the pain and hurt washed together, the loss of

Audrey and our parents. I'd been wrong. I'd thought like a kid all this time. Assumed. It didn't bring them back, but it made it... easier.

I finally pushed Rob away and shoved my hands in my pockets. I'd wished I'd talked to Rob years ago, but I'd stayed away. So much time I'd been wrong, that I'd been angry at myself. That I thought Rob hated me. Blamed me.

I cleared my throat. "I called Shefield's heir."

"Yeah?"

"Yeah. He left his property to a niece. She's in graduate school for music. Seemed nice. She's not sure what she's going to do with the place but knows about Markle's offer. I told her I'd match or beat any offer he made."

"Are you serious?" Rob studied my face in surprise. "With what money?"

"Dude. How can you not have noticed?" I pointed to my huge belt buckle. "I am a fucking *world champion* bull rider. I've made a fortune, and I haven't spent a dime. I figured the time would come when I'd find an investment that interested me."

Rob peered at me. "And this is it? Buying the ranch next door?"

"She said she had no interest in selling to anyone, so we don't have to worry about Markle getting the land."

He slapped me on the shoulder. "See, you're dealing with Markle. I never would have thought of contacting Shefield's heir. Since she's not selling, you still going to settle here? I thought you couldn't wait to get away from Cooper Valley."

I picked up another stone but didn't throw it. I rolled it around between my fingers. "Truth is, I couldn't wait to get away from here. From our parents' death and feeling like a fuck-up. Turned out, no matter how far I traveled, it never went away."

Rob shook his head. "Boyd, I am sorry if I ever made you feel that way."

I knocked the hat off his head. "Yeah, you did. All the fucking time."

He stooped to pick it up. "Well, I didn't mean it. I'm just an asshole with everyone. My job as alpha isn't to be everyone's best friend. I have to make decisions others might not like. But that's me. You, Boyd? You're the one with the brightest future. You could do anything. You proved it on the rodeo circuit, but I guess I always wondered when you were gonna start really living."

My chest tightened painfully. I was starting now. For Audrey. If she would just take me back.

"Fuck off," I muttered.

Rob chuckled and slapped me hard on the back. "So what are you going to do to win that female of yours back?"

What, indeed?

Wait... I turned and faced him head on. "Does that mean you'll let me mate her?"

Rob scoffed. "I might stop you from fucking up your life with a human, but if your wolf chose Audrey, then I won't stand in your way. Besides, there's no way anyone could ever stop you from doing what you wanted to do. Especially not me."

"You kicking me out of the pack?" I asked, but I already knew he wasn't.

He rubbed the back of his neck and settled his Stetson back on his head. "You sure she's your mate?"

I narrowed my gaze, and even he could hear my wolf growl. "Fucking positive. My teeth already came down to mark her. I'm telling you, I knew it the minute I saw her."

"Lucky bastard."

I had to wonder if his moon madness was affecting him. Was he searching for his mate and yet I'd found mine?

"If she's your mate, then she's part of the pack, too," he stated. "Just as soon as you win her back. Don't fuck this up again, fuck-up."

I punched him in the shoulder. For once, I didn't have the anger, the bad feelings when I stood with my brother. I felt... whole. So I replied with all the piss and vinegar of a kid brother. "Asshole.

25

Audrey

Six letters. Boyd wrote me six letters.

They were all in my trash. Who was I fooling? I hadn't taken out the garbage all week. If I was really done with Boyd, wouldn't I have burned them? Or never even brought them in?

I stared at the wastebasket.

Don't do it.

Do *not* do it.

My phone rang. Shoot. It was Marina. I'd been dodging her calls all week because I knew if we talked, I'd spill everything. I sent this call to voicemail as well. She was used to my work schedule and sometimes a lapse in responses, but I'd text her, let her know not to worry.

Because if I talked to her now, I'd bawl my eyes out. Other than the day we broke up, when I lost it out front, I'd been trying to hold that mess in. I'd done a good job of it, but I was like a pressure cooker, ready to explode.

I stooped and picked out the envelopes from the trash can. I'd had six days to think about it.

To remember all the tiny things. The gentle way Boyd put my glasses back on for me after riding the mechanical bull. The rough way he lost control with me when we had sex, as if he couldn't hold himself back. The respectful way he always treated me—opening doors and escorting me home. But more than that because those were superficial things, I kept thinking about the story about his parents. How deeply he hurt over their deaths.

Most of all, I remembered how sure he was that I was *The One*. Whatever that meant to a wolf.

As much as I tried not to, I kept thinking about the fact that he *was* a wolf. There were dynamics at play I didn't understand. Their customs. The culture. He'd briefly mentioned how they operated in a pack and how his brother's disapproval of our relationship would be a big problem for him, considering how much he already felt like a screw-up. While he was a grown man, he still had to take the pack into account when being with someone like me. Someone human.

He had used sex as a weapon. He'd used it to distract me from trying to figure out how a guy who had a sucking chest wound could be healed in such a short time. How his injury had completely disappeared in days. Well, probably sooner, but when the bandage had come off, his skin had been blemish free. Had everything we'd done been at his brother's orders? Maybe he'd had to distract me, but perhaps he was the one who got distracted. Maybe he'd actually fallen in love.

Did wolves fall in love or was that all an act, too? I just didn't know.

A heavy knock sounded at my door, making me jump back from the trashcan and shriek.

"Doctor Ames?" It was a deep, gruff voice that came through the front door. But not Boyd's.

Disappointment crushed my chest. God. I hadn't realized how much I'd hoped he'd show up until now. I'd told myself I wouldn't see him if he had, but that was a lie.

I'd secretly wanted Boyd to come here and win me back. It was too bad he was so damn respectful of my wishes.

I opened the door a crack and sucked in a breath.

Rob. Boyd's brother.

He took off his hat and held it in front of his chest. "Dr. Ames, could I have a word with you? Just for a minute?"

I tried and failed to swallow, then nodded and stepped back.

"Oh, I don't need to come in," he said, his gaze falling to the stack of unopened letters in my hand.

I tried to throw them back in the trash, but my fingers wouldn't open, so instead, I tucked my arm behind my back to hide them. I didn't know why—he'd already seen them and probably knew with some wolf sense that they were from Boyd.

"Dr. Ames, I just wanted to try to clear some things up. Some misunderstandings."

"O-okay."

"My brother's in love with you."

I stopped breathing.

"Yes, I asked him to keep an eye on you since you'd seen him get hurt at the rodeo, but you see, Boyd was only too happy to comply with his alpha's orders for once in his life.

Because getting close to you was the only thing on his mind."

Oh shit. I was going to cry. I did not want to cry in front of Rob. I blinked furiously.

"It's true Boyd was quite the womanizer in the past. But it's different with you. He... smiles. He's the real Boyd. Most of all, he doesn't just take my shit, even if I am the alpha. I know because I'm also his brother."

For some reason my fingers decided to go slack, and the envelopes clattered to the floor behind me. Rob looked down at them. His expression was hard to read, but I thought I detected sympathy there. Whether it was for Boyd or for me, I wasn't sure.

"I don't know if he explained to you how mating works for our kind?"

My heart started pounding. I gave a tiny, frantic shake of my head.

"Wolves mate for life. According to the lore, there's only one female who will give a wolf the instinct to mate. Wolves who don't find their mate by a certain age... " He scrubbed a hand over his face. "They can go moon mad. They become more and more feral until they lose their humanity completely. It's dangerous, see. Many wolves don't wait for the mating instinct, they choose a suitable female and start a family. Much like humans, I'm sure."

Goosebumps stood up on my arms. Yes, it was like humans, minus the part about having one true mate. Although I guessed some humans believed in that, too.

"Wh-why are you telling me all this?" I asked, pushing my glasses up although he couldn't miss the way my hand shook.

"You're Boyd's true mate."

"He never said that."

"Did he say you were his, that he knew all along, from the very first, that he wanted you?"

I nodded, tears lodged thick in my throat.

"He didn't use the word *mate* because he couldn't share about his wolf. His wolf chose a human, for whatever reason. *You.* And while that's generally against pack law, I would never presume to know better than the wolf instinct. Nature always knows best, right? I know Boyd, and he's a stubborn bastard. There's no way he would accept any female but you. So if you refuse him…"

I finally picked up what Rob was putting down. A giant sticky guilt trip. "He'll go moon mad."

"Right."

I needed to be alone. I needed to think things over.

And yes, I might need to read those letters.

So I swung the door shut.

"Just think about seeing him?" he called out, just before I shut the door in his face. On the alpha. Of the Wolf pack.

I didn't answer.

My head spun.

Or was that the room?

Whatever it was, I needed to sit down. Or maybe I needed an oxygen mask. Yes, an oxygen mask would be perfect right now. I sank to the floor and gathered the letters up in my lap.

An oxygen mask, or maybe a letter that I had a feeling had every answer I'd wanted for the past two days.

MARINA: *Call me or I will drive there and track you down.*

. . .

Marina's text got me off the floor. Well, at least from lying on the floor with Boyd's letters strewn around me. I pushed up and leaned against the couch and grabbed my cell. It had been two hours since Rob left—not that I gave him any choice with the front door in his face—and I'd read through Boyd's letters over and over.

I knew his heart now. I knew... everything. He'd written long letters, telling me how he felt about me. What it meant that his wolf had chosen me. That he wanted to mate me... for life. He explained how a wolf marked his mate. What it would mean for me, as a human. He said the pack would accept me because his brother would. I held the letters to my chest, letting it all reverberate there. It was so much. It was everything.

Yet I was still sitting here. Alone.

Marina: Now.

I dialed, and she answered on the first ring.

"What's wrong?" she asked right away.

"I'm in love," I replied, then burst into tears.

I heard Marina laugh, but I couldn't stop crying. I had no idea how long I cried, or why my sister stayed on the phone listening to me gasp and sniffle, sob and blow my nose. When I finally stopped, she said, "Are you crying because you're happy or sad?"

"I don't know!" I wailed.

"Is this about the guy with the weird name who ordered you lamb?"

"Jett? No, not him."

"It's the rodeo champ, right? *Please* say it's the rodeo champ."

"It's the rodeo champ."

She screamed, and I had to pull my phone away from my ear.

"Why are you crying? Did he hurt you? I'll come up there and beat the crap out of him."

Marina and I looked nothing alike, but she wasn't any bigger than me. In fact, she was the same height, but had the slim build of a dancer. A strong wind would blow her over. Not that Boyd would hurt her, but she couldn't even reach his throat without a step stool to punch him there.

"I'm crying because he loves me, too."

I realized that I couldn't tell her that he was a wolf. She'd think I was mental, first off. Then she'd come up here to have me committed. I wanted her in California, in college, where she belonged. I could understand why Rob wanted to ensure their being shifters remained a secret. Keeping Marina far from Montana would ensure she didn't learn the truth. She'd have to come here someday, but I'd worry about that then.

"Then what is going on? I don't understand why you're so upset."

"We had a... falling out." I told her about Karen, skipping the fact that she was a shifter. "I shouldn't have believed her spiteful words, but it's hard not to. You should see her. She looks like a Victoria's Secret model."

"Yet Boyd loves *you*."

"Yeah, he does." Having Marina say it somehow made things shift inside me. Rob had said the exact same thing earlier, yet I'd felt just as bad. Just as heartsick.

Boyd loved me. *Boyd loved me.* He didn't say the words aloud. He hadn't had to. I saw how he felt for me in everything he did. In how he protected me. In how he touched me. How he spoke to me. Fucked me.

In his letters, he hadn't said it either. In fact, he'd emptied his heart to me in those six notes. Everything except those three words. He said if I took him back, that he'd share them with me. Say them, so I could hear them from his lips. Believe them.

"Marina... I have to go."

"To see Boyd?"

"Yes. I have to go right now."

"I'm coming out to meet him! In fact, I'm booking my flight now!"

I gave a watery laugh as I hung up on her, and I could hear her shouts of happiness. I hopped up from the floor and ran to my car. I'd waited my whole life for a man to be mine, to make a family with. A life with. I had it with Boyd. I just had to go and get it.

26

Boyd

My mother used to say plan for the outcome you wanted to achieve—even if it seemed unlikely to happen at the time. When I hit puberty and was pissed off that I hadn't had my first shift yet, she would pull me down to sit beside her and say, "Let's plan the party we're going to have to celebrate your first shift." And then I started making a list of all the things I wanted to do at my party, which was mostly about food because I was a growing pup and could eat the entire refrigerator's contents in one sitting. We made a list of all the food I wanted at the party: pizza and hamburgers and chocolate cupcakes. We talked about who I wanted to invite: just family and the ranchers, not the rest of the pack. By the time we were done, my mood had changed from resistance to anticipation.

It had been wise then, and I tried it now.

Audrey hadn't taken me back, but I was planning for

when she did. I'd told Rob I was claiming one of the ranch's private cabins as my own. No way would I claim my mate in my childhood bedroom in the main house. He'd nodded in agreement, and that was that. I'd gone up there, to the one our grandparents used to live in before they died and began to clean it out.

Besides a good scrubbing, it needed some upgrades—granite countertops in the kitchen, some nice Italian marble in the bathroom. The floors were a beautiful tongue and groove oak plank. All they needed was to be sanded and refinished. The walls—hmm. I'd have to wait for Audrey to take me back to make decisions about the walls. I didn't know if she'd like them to remain rustic, with the logs showing the way they were now, or if I should cover them in plaster and let her pick paint colors.

I would do all the work, of course.

She worked hard enough.

So far, I'd spotlessly cleaned the place and had a new king-sized bed delivered, complete with the best mattress and real linen sheets. I'd yet to have her in a bed and fantasized about what I'd do to her first.

Like planning my first shift party, getting in the mode of imagining how I would trick this cabin out until it met every last one of Audrey's dreams lightened my mood.

Hope started to bleed in.

Enthusiasm for the future I imagined for us. Together. Mated.

This cabin was for us, for the family I would give her. Hell, it was the first place that was really *mine*. I'd left home and pretty much lived in hotel rooms ever since. It felt good to stand here, to know this was where I'd live with Audrey for the rest of our lives.

First, she had to take me back. Second, I had to mate her.

I'd had a long talk with Rob about the mating bite, and he thought I could fight the instinct to tear her flesh and keep my human consciousness enough to choose a safe enough place on her body where I didn't bite too deep. Audrey was a doctor, and I'd get her thoughts on it... assuming she'd be okay with it. I had to hope that since she didn't seem bothered by the fact that I was a shifter that she'd be okay with this, too. She'd know muscle density and shit. The bite would hurt her—and I fucking hated that part because she wouldn't heal quick like a wolf—but it wouldn't kill her.

I was getting too far ahead of myself, and I closed my eyes, took a breath. Calmed myself and my wolf. I'd get her back, I just had to have patience. For a guy whose job lasted eight seconds at a time, it was fucking hard.

I heard the crunch of gravel and stepped out to see who it was. The cabin was built on a bluff over the first rise from the main house. It had views of the mountains to the south and practically all of Montana to the north. The road that led to it dead ended at the cabin, so no one ever drove out this way. I recognized Rob's truck and—oh fates—Audrey sat beside him.

My wolf stood up and practically howled at the sight of her. I couldn't help the grin that split my face, the way my heart skipped a beat then pounded. It was as if seeing her brought me back to life. Yeah, I loved Audrey, and that was never going to change.

I wanted to race to the truck and throw the door open, scoop her into my arms and carry her across the threshold like a groom carrying his bride. But no. She wasn't mine yet.

The last thing she told me was not to call her.

I had to stand here and wait. Wait for her to show me a sign first.

A shiver of recognition, of anticipation, ran through me

as I stood rooted to the porch, watching her. Her peach scent tickled my nose the moment she stepped out of the truck. Rob didn't get out. Hell, he didn't even turn off the engine, only tipped his hat and drove off, leaving her here with me.

Alone. Together. If she was done with me, it was a mile back to the ranch house.

Audrey fumbled with her purse and then dropped it like she was nervous. She bent, as if to pick it up, then seemed to change her mind. Stood. I caught my breath as I realized she was running.

Toward me.

Into my arms, which I stretched wide to catch her. She flung herself at me and wrapped her legs around my waist, her arms around my neck. I hooked my forearm under her ass and buried my face in her neck. Breathed her in. If she thought I was ever letting her go now, she was sorely mistaken.

My wolf sighed, and I exhaled a deep breath. She felt warm and soft, fragrant and sweet.

"Boyd," she choked, her warm breath fanning my neck. It sent goosebumps along my skin. "Thank you for the letters."

I took care not to squeeze her as tightly as I wanted to. "Did you just now read them?" Fuck, I sounded a little choked up myself. I'd had a feeling she hadn't read them. Maybe just because I didn't want to believe she could've read them and still refused to see me. I'd poured my heart and soul into them... the words just for her.

"Yes." Her arms wound tight around my neck, and she trembled a little, but I didn't scent her tears.

I spun around and carried her inside—yes, across the threshold—then shut the door and pushed her back up against it. She was so close I could see her pale eyes dilate. Her scent changed with hints of her musky arousal.

"Do you believe that you're mine now?" My gaze dropped to her lips. I remembered how she tasted and wanted my fill, but I needed her answer first. "That you're my mate?"

"I might," she whispered against my temple.

I ground the bulge of my cock between her legs. "Then I'll just have to convince you," I rumbled.

"Oh yeah?" Her voice was pure honey. Seductive and sweet. There was a confidence to it she didn't usually have when we were sexual. She hadn't held back with me before, but it seemed like she'd finally realized her power over me. "How are you going to do that, champ?"

"First, I'm going to lay you down on our mating bed." I recaptured her full weight again and carried her toward the large bedroom.

A little V formed in her brow. "Our what?"

"Oh, I guess I'm gettin' ahead of myself, aren't I? See, I was renovating this cabin, thinking I might talk you into living here with me. Making this ours, where we'll raise our pups. There's a big tree out front for that tire swing we talked about. That hill you rode up is the perfect sledding hill. Of course, if you want to live in town to be closer to the hospital, I'll buy you a house there, too."

She gave a watery laugh and kissed my neck. "I think you're still ahead of yourself with the tire swing, but I'd like to know more about this mating bed."

"Mmm. Well, it's this one right here." I laid her down on it, her dark hair fanning out on the white blanket. "A brand-new king-sized love pad just for you." I unbuttoned her shorts and dragged them down her thighs with her panties.

Got rid of her sandals. "And right now, I'm going to use it to show you the treatment I want you to get used to."

"Shouldn't we... talk?"

I stilled, my gaze shifting from her pussy to her face. "Are you leaving me?"

"No."

"Do you love me?"

She licked her lips. "Yes."

"Say it," I all but growled. My wolf wanted to hear the words from her lips.

"Boyd Wolf, I love you."

I'd never felt better in my life than right now. My mate loved me. She was in our bed, her pussy bare and ready to be claimed.

"Audrey Ames, I didn't say it in the letters. I wanted to look you in the eye, just as I am now, so you could hear the truth. See it on my face. I love you."

Tears slipped from her eyes, and she smiled.

Fuck yes.

"Talking's over," I said, tossing my hat to the floor. Using my shoulders, I pushed her knees wide and licked into her, one long lap with a flat tongue, then another.

"Boyd!"

I growled as her taste coated my tongue. Her scent filled my head. Her soft skin was beneath my palms. My dick was uncomfortable in my jeans, but it could wait. I had to please my mate first. I settled in and used the pointy tip of my tongue to trace inside her labia, around her clit.

She squeaked and moaned and shifted around, her belly shuddering with each breath, her fingers finding my hair. Tangling. Tugging.

"You see, a wolf can't ever leave his mate," I told her when I lifted my head to look at her beautiful face. Her essence coated my mouth and chin. Her cheeks had flushed pink, and her eyes were closed, but they flew open when I spoke. "It's biologically impossible. But she can leave him. So that means his one job in life is to make sure she stays happy."

Color feathered across Audrey's chest, her blue eyes shone bright. "This is how you're going to do that?"

I fucking loved the breathy way she spoke.

I flicked my tongue over her clit again. "That's right. I'm going to lick your pussy every damned day. Among other things."

"Show me," she commanded, gripping my head and pushing my face into her wet folds.

A snarl rose up in my chest, taking me by surprise. Fuck. The full moon was just a few days away. Making love to Audrey without marking her might be an impossibility.

I shoved my wolf down as best I could.

Right now was about making Audrey feel good, and I was going to do that if it killed me. I flicked my tongue over her clit in a steady series of flicks, then used my thumb to retract the hood so I could suck it.

Audrey screamed, her hips bobbing beneath me. "Oh my God, Boyd!" She shoved me off her. "Boyd. *Boyd.*" I lifted my head.

"I need you inside me. Please."

Hell, yes.

She didn't need to ask me twice.

I stood up on my knees to pull a condom from my pocket.

She held up her hand. "No condom."

I frowned, froze.

"I want you bare."

"There's no fucking way I'm pulling out." I was strong,

but not that strong. I'd never gone without a condom before. Ever. Feeling Audrey's pussy, all hot and wet against my uncovered dick... I wasn't even sure how long I'd last. I'd probably go off like a randy kid and embarrass myself. But I sure as fuck wasn't going to be able to pull out.

"Good."

I opened my jeans, pushed them down enough, so I could pull out my dick. I gripped the base, stroked it from root to tip as I stared down at my mate. Pre-cum beaded, then slid down the crown.

"You want my cum in you?"

She bit her lip and watched as I squeezed the base, hard, to stave off coming all over her belly. "Yes."

"You know what's going to happen?"

She looked up at me. "I'm an ObGyn. I'd say I have a pretty good idea."

I shut my eyes, tried to block out how fucking hot she looked. My mate was finally with me, and I was holding off. I had to though.

"Audrey," I groaned.

"I love you," she said. "I want it all with you. Why wait?"

Setting a hand beside her head, I leaned down. Kissed her. I tried to go as calmly and as sweetly as possible, but her words, the fact that she wanted me to put a baby in her belly, was making it almost impossible to remain calm.

"Your eyes are glowing," she whispered when I lifted my head. "Is that the wolf?"

I stroked her cheek, amazed at how silky soft it felt. "Yeah, darlin'. Did you, ah, read my letter about... marking? The way a wolf takes his mate?"

Her glasses were crooked on her face, and I reached to carefully take them off.

"I read it."

"You want a baby, we'll give it to you. But my wolf wants to claim you. Right now. On our mating bed. Besides filling you with my cum, it also means puncturing your skin. It's forever, darlin'."

She raised her arms to lift her shirt, and I stood back up to give her room. She got the shirt up and off and cupped her breasts through her bra. "I want to be claimed," she purred. "I want your cum in me. I want *you*."

"Are you sure?" I asked again, helping her strip off her bra next. It was one thing to have consent to fuck, another entirely to mate.

Perhaps she had a wolf in her because she all but pounced up to her knees and grabbed my dick. Her mouth was over the flared head and licking off all the pre-cum.

"Fuck!" I shouted, my hands instinctively going to her head.

She gave me a strong suck, then pulled off, looked up at me.

"I'm sure."

Jesus fuck! My wolf roared. I stripped in seconds, then dove on top of her, kissing the hell out of her mouth. My teeth were already descending. My vision had sharpened.

The change in her was remarkable. Before, she'd surrendered to my sexual advances. Her body had been responsive, her passion deep and her kink was definitely wild, but she'd been unsure of me. Of us. Now, she'd come into her power.

"You finally believe me," I said, nudging her knees apart and settling into the space between. My cock slid over her wet folds, coating it.

"About what?" She rolled her hips in eagerness.

"About how fucking sexy I find you. How beautiful. How

incredible. I don't give a shit about Karen or any other woman. Human or shifter. Now or ever. Got me?"

"Yes."

I dropped down on top of her and kissed her mouth again. My rigid cock found her entrance without my hand to guide it. I rocked gently and—fuck!— it inched in. My eyes rolled back in my head at the exquisite feel of taking her bare. The tight clench of her pussy, how her sticky arousal coated the head of my dick, how my pre-cum was already beginning to mark her. From now on, any shifter would scent me all over her. My teeth came down again.

She felt so good, and I only had the tip in. I was thrusting before I meant to even move, claiming her so hard the bed slammed against the log wall. Fuck—I didn't want to hurt her.

"Yes, Boyd," she encouraged, her nails digging into my shoulders. "Harder."

Fates, if she kept it up, I'd lose my mind before we even got started. I'd blow my load before she got off.

Speaking of mind—I needed to concentrate. Except it was getting harder and harder. My hips had found a delicious rhythm rocking in and out of her, stroking inside her tight channel with the most satisfying thrusts. The wet sounds of my dick fucking her pussy filled the air.

"Where... where do you want it?" I panted, trying hard to stay focused.

Her blurry eyes looked up at me and she frowned. "It's in me."

I couldn't help but grin. "My bite, darlin'. You tell me where it should go, so it's not so bad for you."

In the letters, I mentioned the mating bite, about what Rob and I had discussed about making it safe for her. I told her as a doctor, she would know best where I should leave my mark.

"Oh, the bite?" She lifted her shoulder, let it drop. "Right here, in my deltoid. That should be safest."

I closed my eyes and nodded, trying to keep my cool. This was the moment, like saying vows when getting married. I'd dreamed of this, hoped for it, but never expected I'd find my mate. That she'd love me back, give me everything, including a baby. A pup.

I brought my thumb to her clit. I'd bite her during her climax, hoping it would minimize the pain. She liked it rough, and I had to hope maybe it might even make it hotter for her. I wouldn't bite her again, but I'd sure as fuck know if she were into playing with the whole pleasure in pain thing in the future. Spanking that juicy ass of hers had been pure heaven. She'd loved it, dripped down her thighs from it.

She was holding back, though, watching me. When I flicked an eyebrow, she panted, "I want to come when you do."

I grinned, pulled my thumb from her clit. I liked her idea better than mine.

"All right, darlin'. Let's do this."

I laced my fingers over hers and held her hands down by her head, rocking, rocking, rocking into her. I fucked her harder and harder. Faster, ensuring I ground down against her clit with each thrust. Then I slowed it back down. Twice more I brought the tempo and intensity up, then down. I hadn't planned a pattern or a rhythm. I hadn't even thought I'd make it this long without losing control, but the sex was too good to stop.

I hovered my face over hers as I continued to pound into her. Looked down at her. Met her gaze. Held it. "I love you, Audrey Ames."

Her face contorted as if in pain, and then she came, her pussy squeezing around my cock.

That was what did me in. I came, too, a beast-like roar ripping from my throat as my balls tightened, and I shot my load. I kept pumping, pumping hard and focused on the meat of her shoulder muscle, where she wanted me to bite.

Be gentle, I warned my wolf. But he'd already agreed because I was in total control as I lowered my head and opened my jaws. I punctured her flesh with the top two canines. She screamed and writhed beneath me, her pussy milking the cum from my balls. Every drop of it.

Knowing it was filling her up, not a condom, combined with the heat of her, the perfect sense of making her mine had my head practically exploding.

It was possible I'd gone blind with pleasure.

I'd never come like this before, having everything I ever wanted in one perfect moment.

I tasted her blood and released my hold, relaxing my jaw and licking the wounds to help them close and heal.

She moaned and writhed beneath me, her pussy still pulsing around me. Cum seeped out around my dick even though I stayed buried deep. Our skin was slick with sweat, her nipples hard peaks pressed into my chest. Her cheeks were flushed, and I'd never seen her look so beautiful.

She was mine.

"Audrey, darlin'. Are you okay? Talk to me."

"It was nothing," she said, as if surprised, then gave a relieved laugh. She was smiling.

I resumed my slow thrusts inside her because it still felt too good to stop, and I was still hard. More and more cum slipped from her, making us a sticky mess. I didn't give a shit. Just knowing she was marked, that my cum filled her womb and that we may have made a pup...

Eventually I slid out and dropped to my side beside her. I licked her wound again because my saliva had healing properties. I hadn't torn the flesh as I'd expected, only two small puncture marks were visible.

"I love you." I stroked the side of her face. "I'm sorry I hurt you."

Her eyes filled with tears, and she turned her head to look at me. "You didn't hurt me, Boyd. I hurt myself wasting days of being apart. I never should've believed a word Karen said. I got the bitch vibe from her back in the bar. I just... I'm not used to being pursued by men, and she's gorgeous. It seemed easy to believe you'd been faking it with me the whole time."

I held up my hand like I was swearing an oath. "Never faked it. Never once. Fuck, I had it for you from the very start. You're the only female for me." I grabbed a handful of tissues from the nightstand and held them over her puncture marks. "This bite ensured that."

Audrey let out a wobbly laugh. "This is all so crazy. I can't believe I just married a guy I met less than ten days ago. And I can't believe that guy is a werewolf."

"Shifter." I grinned. "That's the preferred term. What we just did?" I cupped her pussy, coated my fingers in my cum and spread it all over. "This seed, that bite, they mean forever. You're good and claimed. But I'll give you a wedding. Darlin', I will buy you the biggest diamond—or the smallest," I amended when she made a face. "I'll buy you the perfect wedding ring. Whatever you've always dreamed of. And I'm gonna give you that picket fence. Family. Pups. Stability. Sex. Undying love. We're gonna have it all, Doc. You name it, I'll provide it."

Audrey's eyes filled with tears. "I love you, Boyd Wolf.

You're not the guy I thought I'd marry." My heart stuttered for a moment, but she went on, "You're so much better."

I cupped her face and kissed her softly this time, a slow, sensual gliding of lips over lips, a light stroking of my tongue. I was hard and ready to go for round two. If she wanted a baby, I was going to do everything in my power to give her one.

When I broke the kiss, she gazed at me with heavy lids. "Show me your wolf."

27

Audrey

A SLOW SMILE spread across Boyd's face. "You wanna see my wolf?"

"Yes. What color are you? Brown? Silver? Black?" She reached out, stroked my hair. "I'm thinking light."

"Silver. With blue eyes. I'll show you. Don't be afraid, all right? I won't hurt you." He closed his eyes and turned his face into the mattress, and in the next moment, I heard the crack and snap of bones, like I'd heard at the swimming hole.

I gasped as Boyd's human form transformed into the biggest wolf I'd ever seen, right there on the bed beside me. I sat up. Stared.

Even though I knew it was Boyd, my initial instinct was to back away. I could see why he'd warned me before he shifted. The great silver wolf lowered his head and whined, licking my face.

All my fear dropped away. I laughed and reached for him, running my hands over his soft fur. "You're beautiful. Terrifying, but beautiful."

He licked my face again. I continued to stroke him, paying attention to his silky ears. His head leaned in, and I realized it was something he really liked. I couldn't help but admire his wild beauty. I pressed my face into his neck. He still smelled like Boyd. Strong and masculine. And wild.

I was in awe. "You're incredible, Boyd. Magnificent."

He shifted back and pulled me into his arms. "I'm sorry I frightened you. Don't ever be scared of me or my wolf, Audrey. Our one job in life is to protect you and keep you happy. I promise."

It felt too good to be true.

Only this time, I believed Boyd. He'd never given me any reason to doubt him, even though I had. I'd been wrong. So very wrong. Now I had forever to make it up to him. To prove I loved him right back.

I nestled into his chest, ran my fingernails through the light fur there. "I'm yours now?"

"What we just did didn't convince you?" he asked, his thumb brushing over my nipple. "Forever, darlin'. You can't get rid of me."

"I won't want to," I promised. I was sure of it. Boyd Wolf was perfect and all mine. "I love you, Boyd Wolf."

"I love you, too, darlin'. Always."

Ready for more Wolf Ranch?
Get Wolf Ranch: Wild next!

Pack Rule #2: Always protect your mate

I protected my country. Protected my platoon.
Now all I wanted to protect was *her*.
Too bad that wasn't an option.
I couldn't fall for the beautiful slip of a female.
The baby sister of my brother's new mate.
She was way too young. Way too human.
Still in college. And too bright a force of nature.
She had her whole life ahead of her.
And I had the Green Berets begging me to reenlist.
But my wolf... he wanted her.
But if I let her go without claiming her,
I might not survive the moon madness.

Get Wolf Ranch: Wild !

NOTE FROM VANESSA & RENEE

Guess what? We've got some bonus content for you with Audrey and Boyd. Yup, there's more!

Click here to read more!
or go to this link:
http://vanessavaleauthor.com/v/1ei

WANT FREE RENEE ROSE BOOKS?

Go to http://subscribepage.com/alphastemp to sign up for Renee Rose's newsletter and receive a free copy of *Alpha's Temptation, Theirs to Protect, Owned by the Marine, Theirs to Punish, The Alpha's Punishment, Disobedience at the Dressmaker's* and *Her Billionaire Boss*. In addition to the free stories, you will also get bonus epilogues, special pricing, exclusive previews and news of new releases.

GET A FREE VANESSA VALE BOOK!

Join my mailing list to be the first to know of new releases, free books, special prices and other author giveaways.

http://freeromanceread.com

OTHER TITLES BY RENEE ROSE

Chicago Bratva

"Prelude" in Black Light: Roulette War

The Director

The Fixer

Black Light: Roulette Rematch

The Enforcer

Vegas Underground Mafia Romance

King of Diamonds

Mafia Daddy

Jack of Spades

Ace of Hearts

Joker's Wild

His Queen of Clubs

Dead Man's Hand

Wild Card

More Mafia Romance

Her Russian Master

The Don's Daughter

Mob Mistress

The Bossman

Contemporary

Daddy Rules Series

Fire Daddy

Hollywood Daddy

Stepbrother Daddy

Master Me Series

Her Royal Master

Her Russian Master

Her Marine Master

Yes, Doctor

Double Doms Series

Theirs to Punish

Theirs to Protect

Holiday Feel-Good

Scoring with Santa

Saved

Other Contemporary

Black Light: Valentine Roulette

Black Light: Roulette Redux

Black Light: Celebrity Roulette

Black Light: Roulette War

Black Light: Roulette Rematch

Punishing Portia (written as Darling Adams)

The Professor's Girl

Safe in his Arms

Paranormal

Wolf Ranch Series

Rough

Wild

Feral

Savage

Fierce

Ruthless

Wolf Ridge High Series

Alpha Bully

Alpha Knight

Bad Boy Alphas Series

Alpha's Temptation

Alpha's Danger

Alpha's Prize

Alpha's Challenge

Alpha's Obsession

Alpha's Desire

Alpha's War

Alpha's Mission

Alpha's Bane

Alpha's Secret

Alpha's Prey

Alpha's Sun

Alpha's Moon

Midnight Doms

Alpha's Blood

His Captive Mortal

Alpha Doms Series

The Alpha's Hunger

The Alpha's Promise

The Alpha's Punishment

Other Paranormal

The Winter Storm: An Ever After Chronicle

Sci-Fi

Zandian Masters Series

His Human Slave

His Human Prisoner

Training His Human

His Human Rebel

His Human Vessel

His Mate and Master

Zandian Pet

Their Zandian Mate

His Human Possession

Zandian Brides

Night of the Zandians

Bought by the Zandians

Mastered by the Zandians

Zandian Lights

Kept by the Zandian

Claimed by the Zandian

Stolen by the Zandian

Other Sci-Fi

The Hand of Vengeance

Her Alien Masters

Regency

The Darlington Incident

Humbled

The Reddington Scandal

The Westerfield Affair

Pleasing the Colonel

Western

His Little Lapis

The Devil of Whiskey Row

The Outlaw's Bride

Medieval

Mercenary

Medieval Discipline

Lords and Ladies

The Knight's Prisoner

Betrothed

Held for Ransom

The Knight's Seduction

The Conquered Brides (5 book box set)

Renaissance

Renaissance Discipline

ALSO BY VANESSA VALE

For the most up-to-date listing of my books, go to:

vanessavalebooks.com

All Vanessa Vale titles are available at Apple, Google, Kobo, Barnes & Noble, Amazon and other retailers worldwide.

ABOUT RENEE ROSE

USA TODAY BESTSELLING AUTHOR RENEE ROSE loves a dominant, dirty-talking alpha hero! She's sold over a half million copies of steamy romance with varying levels of kink. Her books have been featured in USA Today's *Happily Ever After* and *Popsugar*. Named Eroticon USA's Next Top Erotic Author in 2013, she has also won *Spunky and Sassy's* Favorite Sci-Fi and Anthology author, *The Romance Reviews* Best Historical Romance, and *Spanking Romance Reviews'* Best Sci-fi, Paranormal, Historical, Erotic, Ageplay and favorite couple and author. She's hit the *USA Today* list five times with various anthologies.

Please follow her on:
Bookbub | Goodreads

Renee loves to connect with readers!
www.reneeroseromance.com
reneeroseauthor@gmail.com

ABOUT VANESSA VALE

Vanessa Vale is the *USA Today* bestselling author of sexy romance novels, including her popular Bridgewater historical series and hot contemporary romances. With over one million books sold, Vanessa writes about unapologetic bad boys who don't just fall in love, they fall hard. Her books are available worldwide in multiple languages in e-book, print, audio and even as an online game. When she's not writing, Vanessa savors the insanity of raising two boys and figuring out how many meals she can make with a pressure cooker. While she's not as skilled at social media as her kids, she loves to interact with readers.

BookBub

Instagram

- facebook.com/vanessavaleauthor
- twitter.com/iamvanessavale
- instagram.com/vanessa_vale_author
- bookbub.com/profile/vanessa-vale

Printed in Great Britain
by Amazon